# 2030 Predicted Victory

2030 PREDICTED VICTORY

**First edition. June 30, 2024.**



ISBN: 979-8227475732

Written by Yeong Hwan Choi.

# 2030 Predicted Victory

Written by Younghwan Choi
**Email** ◈ cyhchs12@naver.com

# Table of Contents

# <2030 Republic of Korea>

News Reporter: "This is in front of the Capitol. Once again, the corruption cases of lawmakers were distributed through various social media and portals. Thousands of angry citizens are demonstrating in front of the Parliament building, and clashes with police continue."

Protesters: (holding placards) "Down with corruption! Establish justice!"

Police: "Disperse the protesters! Stop the illegal assembly immediately!"

News Reporter: "The government is still ignoring the voices of citizens. Some groups are shouting that the current separation of powers system has collapsed, and that the legislative takeover and monopoly of the executive and judiciary cannot be tolerated."

AG Telecom's headquarters skyscraper, the logo of the building shines in the night view. Han Sung-jun stands looking out the window during the protest.

Han Sung-jun: "Korea is in a very bad place. I don't know where the hell is this country going?"

Secretary Lee Jun-ho urgently knocks on the door and enters.

Secretary Lee Jun-ho: Mr. Vice Chairman, this is a big deal. I received a call from Sungjin Hospital that he was in danger. You'll have to hurry up.

Han Sungjun turns his head in surprise and immediately picks up his jacket and leaves. Escorted by secretaries, they walk through the long corridors of the hospital and arrive at the hospital room. In the intensive care unit, Chairman Han Dong-wook is lying around, surrounded by doctors and family members.

Chairman Han Dong-wook: (in a faint voice) Sung Jun-ah...Come closer.

Vice Chairman Han Sung-joon approaches the bedside. Chairman Han Dong-wook squeezes his son's hand.

Chairman Han Dong-wook: This country. It's already a country that's on the wane, so AG Telecom needs to go in a new direction. There are immutable laws in the world...It's time to make a choice.

"In the midst of a crisis.... Opportunities lurk...."

Han Sung-jun's eyes fill with tears. Chairman Han quietly closes his eyes, and the room goes silent.

Amid the extravagant funeral, political figures from all walks of life made their way through the crowd of protesters. Han Sung-jun stands alone, dressed in a black suit and greeting mourners. His father's words on his deathbed haunt his mind.

Han Sung-jun: 'Opportunity is hidden in crisis...What did my father mean by that...'

Han Shengjun looked around silently. Political figures were lined up in a triangular formation behind each other, as if to show off their power, and they were still rude here, as was the case with Ahn Hamuin. They offered pretentious words of comfort to Vice Chairman Han Sung-jun, patting him on the shoulder or giving him a shallow smile. Han Shengjun tried his best to be polite and bowed his head, but there was a quiet anger in his eyes.

Member of Parliament: "Mr. Vice Chairman, you have a lot of work to do. Haha."

Congressman 2: "That's right. I'm sorry to be in this position today. He was a wise man."

Han Sungjun: "How much money did I give you? Do you know how you could have been so powerful without me?'

Suppressing resentment and anger, he continued quietly.

Han Sungjun: (inwardly) "with on their heads..."

Han Shengjun let out a deep sigh and looked up. Political figures showed their power without paying attention to the public, and Han smiled wryly.

After the grand funeral, Han Sung-jun is alone and quietly lost in thought.

Han Sung-jun: (monologue) "I'm going to seize this opportunity to become the most powerful person."

In a dark room, several computers are blinking and working. Kim Yoo-jin is looking at the screen and quickly teasing the keyboard. The room is distracting, with coffee cups and snack bags strewn about. On the desk is a jumble of various hacking books and notes with codes.

Kim Yoojin: (talking to himself) "It's going to be fun. Exposing the true nature of corrupt governments and big corporations has made the people seething. It's like a fish in water."

She smiles as she flips through classified government documents on her computer screen. Take off your headphones and stand up with a sigh. She leans against the window, tossing her toes through the bras and panties strewn everywhere. The windows have been closed for a long time, and dust is gathering.

My cell phone rings. The name "Lee Jun-ho" pops up on the screen. Kim Yoo-jin hesitates for a moment and then answers the phone.

Kim Yoojin: (Phone) "Hello?"

Junho Lee: (over the phone) "Yoojin-ah, it's me. It's been a while. How are you doing?"

Kim Yoojin: (in a slightly tired voice) "Junho-senpai. Well, it's always like that. I'm busy running around."

Junho Lee: "Can I see your face? I have something important to talk about."

Kim Yoojin: "Face? (pauses) Okay. I needed to catch my breath anyway."

Junho Lee: "Okay. I'll see you later."

Kim Yoo-jin reaches out to drink the cold coffee that was lying nearby, sits down again, and taps on the keyboard. Differing from the world outside the window, her own little world unfolds in a small 10-square-meter studio.

# Episode 1 Chaos

IN THE WARM SPRING of 2030, a sense of despair was evident on the faces of citizens walking through an alleyway illuminated by the yellow street lights of Seoul. Then, sitting on the terrace of the café on the other side, with only his butt on his buttocks, he hears the conversation of young people.

Young man 1: (clenching his fist) "Politicians, rotten things. Whether it's on the left or the right, they're all looking out for their own interests. People like us don't care."

Young man 2: "That's right. All the policies to solve the problem of the declining birthrate are just a show. There is no real policy for 2030 and the future. It's not people like us that they really care."

Young man 3: "In the conflict between men and women, in the conflict of generations. The economic collapse was ultimately caused by the government and its lawmakers. What the two parties are doing is not a check. Their beatings and fights with each other made our lives more and more exhausted. I don't even want to see the real thing. You've completely split the country in half."

Young Man 1: "They control the executive, legislative, and judicial branches and are busy doing things for themselves. It's time for the people to take matters into their own hands. I can't stand it."

News Studio. The announcer is delivering the news with a serious expression. Behind him, photographs appear with the faces of lawmakers and high-ranking officials. Televisions and smartphones are playing news on electronic billboards on the streets of Gangnam.

Announcer: "Breaking news. Even today, it was revealed that members of the National Assembly, high-ranking government officials, judges, prosecutors, and ministers and vice ministers were involved in corruption such as sexual entertainment and slush funds. Their people, who have been working for the people, are being exposed in detail. The government, the judiciary and the legislature, which have lost the trust of the people, are in great turmoil."

There are empty playgrounds and closed schools. In the silence of Korea, where the cries of children have disappeared, citizens with distorted expressions of discontent are gathering one after another on the streets. On the newsstands, there was a sign on the front door that read, "Exposing the corruption of members of the National Assembly!" It is titled. People are chatting and exchanging their opinions about the situation.

"I don't trust the media. Journalists are splitting sides, and politicians are nothing more than-suckers," a middle-aged man said through gritted teeth.

"Isn't there a reporter who really tells the truth? They're all twisting the truth to suit their own tastes. Who the hell am I supposed to trust?" one woman cried.

"I'd rather someone powerful come along and clean up the National Assembly, the government, and the TV stations. We need someone to fix the Republic of Korea," another man shouts, clenching his fists vigorously.

"yes, we've endured a lot. It's time for action. I can't live in such a corrupt country," the young man says, gritting his teeth.

On every street, people gather together to vent their anger. Posters with the name 'New Korea Movement' were posted everywhere, and citizens nodded their heads in sympathy with the phrase.

"Governments, politicians, and even the media are just trying to get their own food. In spite of our anger, they are deceiving us with a casual face," said an old man with a sad expression.

Their anger is preparing to shake the entire Republic of Korea in a huge wave.

Young man 4: (holding up a megaphone) "One side can't tolerate politics for vested interests! The other side deceives the weak to get votes! Let's change the politicians who are just looking at their faces!"

Citizen 1: "We want a new Korea! We need to fix this country where the cries of children are not heard!"

Citizen 2: "Let's not give a chance to the politicians who have betrayed the people and the opposition who are a group of criminals! We don't need North Korea! Correct South Korea's security and main enemy!"

The crowd becomes more and more numerous, and the voices of anger grow louder. Everywhere you look, you can see people marching with pickets.

Mapo-gu, AG Telecom headquarters skyscraper. The inauguration ceremony of Chairman Han Sung-joon is being held. His face is reflected in the luxurious décor and on the large screen. Employees and key in-house figures clap their hands in congratulations. Han Sung-jun goes up to the stage and gives a speech.

"I'm here today to announce a new beginning. We, AG Telecom, will move forward for a bigger leap forward. We will become a leading company in Korea and the world in the future. I hope you'll join us."

Jung Min-hee, the head of the PR team, listens to Han Sung-jun with a bright smile, as if revealing her lively and outgoing personality. He looks at the audience with a confident expression on his face, watching their reactions carefully.

After the inauguration ceremony, the president's office. In a spacious and modern office, Han Sung-jun stands by the window and looks at the beautiful night view of Gangnam. On the sofa, Chief of Staff Lee Jun-ho and PR Team Leader Jung Min-hee drink coffee.

Han Sung-jun is cold and calculating despite his age in his late 30s. With his piercing eyes and well-groomed appearance, he doesn't show any emotion easily. Lee Jun-ho, who is in his mid-30s and sits on the couch chatting with Jung Min-hee, has been working with Han Sung-joon for a long time and has been his right-hand man. As a pragmatist, he is infinitely loyal to Han Sung-jun, and he also does not show his emotions very well. The pale gray suit he wears always represents his calm personality. He has a great ability to cope with rapidly changing situations, and he is the one who supports Han Sung-jun's ambition more than anyone else.

Han Sungjun: (looking out the window) "In this chaos, whoever holds the information will have the most power."

Junho Lee: "That's right. Mr. Vice President. No Mr. Chairman. What would happen to the world if Google or Apple shut down their services?"

Jung Minhee: "If that means anything, then if the services we provide are stopped, the Republic of Korea will be in an even bigger uproar than it is now."

Jung Min-hee is in her late 30s and has a lively and outgoing personality. A former journalist who is in charge of AG's public relations and communication with the public, she wears a bright blouse and a stylish skirt. Her long hair is neatly tied up and she is always cheerful and smiling.

Han Sungjun: (turning his head) "They say the pen is mightier than the sword. But without the support of that angry crowd, strength alone can't govern the country. What else do you need besides information?"

Jung Min-hee: "We need to find out the existence of hackers who continue to expose politicians with IPs that we can't track. We have a 90% share of the country in social media services and communication networks. But we also need them to find out the information of politicians who use foreign services."

Junho Lee: "Chairman, there are geniuses out there who can control the world with just one PC and a network."

Minhee: "It's important to get in touch with them and draw them in the direction we want them to."

Junho Lee: "That's right, Mr. Chairman. As I mentioned before, there are many hikikomori in their 20s~30s who specialize in one. Among the juniors, there is a junior named Kim Yoo-jin who worked as a white hacker. She left her job at a large U.S. company and is now finding her own path in South Korea."

Han Sungjun: "That's right, Director Lee. We've talked about it before. So how are you preparing for your contact with Kim Yoo-jin?"

Junho Lee: "We're going to meet tonight."

Han Sungjun: "Okay. Lee Joon-ho, Jung Min-hee. We don't have a lot of time."

Han Shengjun stared out the window for a moment, deep in thought. He turns to them again and asks them a meaningful question.

Han Sungjun: "Power.... Is F=ma correct?"

Lee Joon-ho and Jung Min-hee hesitate, as if confused by Han Sung-joon's question.

Junho Lee: "Yes...That's right. Force is the product of mass and acceleration."

Han: "So, as the saying goes, the pen is mightier than the sword, so is information and money stronger than the gun?" (Lost in thought) "Yes. We need something more provocative for the already broken reporters and the people who don't trust the media."

Jung Min-hee and Lee Jun-ho looked at each other and were silent, unable to find an answer.

Han Sungjun: "Director Lee, it's not fun if there aren't dogs and pigs in the country. There's no point in having a lot of money."

Lee Junho looked at Han Sungjun in surprise, and he knew intuitively what he was trying to say.

Han Sung-jun: "The Republic of Korea is going down anyway. Shouldn't we, in this country, who have all the information, give it a try?"

Lee Jun-ho agrees with Han Sung-joon's words, but he can't hide his slight embarrassment at the radicality of his expression. However, he immediately regains his expression and takes Han Sung-jun's words seriously.

Han Sungjun: "If we have both of those things, what's the point of a gun and a knife? I want to show you how we are going to change this country. And we're the ones who can do it!"

Lee Jun-ho nods and accepts his words. Han Sung-jun's ambition penetrates deep into his heart. "Mr. Chairman, I think so. The people will follow us like pigs and dogs. If I can take this country in a new direction, it will be worth it."

Han Sung-jun listened to Lee Jun-ho's words with a satisfied smile and drew his own plan in his head.

Han Sungjun: "Director Lee, you'll be in charge of convincing Kim Yoojin. Let's bring other talents to our side. Let's do a proper sword dance."

Han Sungjun: "And you always need a balance of strength and softness."

Minhee: "So, what we need is...It's the trust and support of the people."

Han Sungjun: "Yes. Without the support of the people, nothing can be done. That's why we need geniuses like Kim Yoo-jin. They're the key to helping us with our plans."

Junho Lee: "Yes, sir. We will make all preparations."

Han Sung-jun: "It's already a damn ruined country."

Lee Jun-ho checks his phone and finds a text message from Kim Yoo-jin. 'Address: XXXX, OO-dong, Gangnam-gu, Seoul.' As soon as I arrived, I knocked on the door, but there was no response. He knocked on the door again. "Kim Yoo-jin! I'm Lee Jun-ho. Are you there?"

When there is still no answer, he turns the knob. "Well, what kind of house does a woman not lock the door in?"

When Lee Jun-ho opens the door and enters, an unpleasant sensation hits his nose, as if the smell of rotten milk and stale air are mixed in the darkness.

"Kim Yoo-jin? Are you here?" he shouts nervously. In one corner, food scraps and used sanitary napkins pile up, and the only light-filled computer monitor is covered in messy cables and empty soda cans.

In the center of the room, Kim Yoo-jin sits in a hoodie, headphones and a hat pressed down. The hoodie looks faded and looks like it has been washed several times, and the long hair that flows under the hat looks like it hasn't been trimmed in a while. His face was pale, and his eyes were dark. His dark eyes are staring at the monitor screen, his eyes devoid of light.

Junho Lee: "Well, are there all these dirty rooms? Can you clean it up?"

Kim Yoo-jin slowly turns her head to look at Lee Joon-ho. His eyes were lethargic, but there was a keen intellect in them. Lee Jun-ho looks at her and remembers how enthusiastic and energetic she was once at school. They majored in computer science at the same university, and Eugene always kept his top grades and got everyone's attention.

Kim Yujin: (smiling bitterly) "Why? I enjoy watching the world fall apart. This chaotic room is perfect for me."

Lee Junho: (Holding his nose) "What the hell is this smell.... Just throw away the sanitary napkins."

Kim Yoojin: (Without taking his eyes off the screen) "Well, it's my style. It's this messy to be able to concentrate."

(There is a moment of silence between the two of them; they are happy to see each other for a moment.)

Lee Junho: "It's been a while. I wondered why you, who were doing so well in America, suddenly disappeared."

Kim Yoojin: "It wasn't fun. Working for a big company isn't my style. It's boring to live by rules. South Korea is full of chaos and fun."

Lee Junho: "But what if he suddenly disappears without any contact? Everybody was worried."

Kim Yoojin: "Who cares about me? After all, it's a life lived alone. But what did you want me to see?"

Lee Jun-ho looks at her trapped in his own world and says with a bitter smile.

Junho Lee: "Why don't you stay in this dark place, get out there and face the world again?"

Kim Yujin replied with a nonchalant shrug.

Kim Yoojin: "What are you asking me to do when I go outside? The world is already ruined, and I don't think there's anything I can do."

Junho Lee: "Why don't you form a team? When the networks we've built and your capabilities are combined, a new world will come."

Kim Yoojin: (Laughing) "Yes, that's right, AG Telecom has taken a cap today. Isn't that too monopolious? Why me, anyway?"

Junho Lee: "If you want to wreak more chaos on the world, you need to join hands with us.

Kim Yoojin: "Hmm...If so, it's going to be even more exciting. What will you give me? If you're going to get a team, you've got to be sure."

Junho Lee: "I can accommodate whatever you want, not to mention money. You're exactly what we need."

Lee Joon-ho nods at Kim Yoo-jin's determined gaze, and the two leave the room, resolving to form a new alliance. Immediately, Kim Yoo-jin focuses on the monitor and taps on the keyboard. Get on the network and try to get in touch with trusted hackers.

Kim Yoo-jin slowly walks to a secluded café that Lee Hyun-woo frequents. As soon as you open the door of the café, you see a man in the corner, tapping away at his laptop. It's Lee Hyun Woo. He has short neatly trimmed hair, wears glasses, and is about 180 cm tall. I was young in my late twenties, but I couldn't help but feel tired with a slight bump on my face. Despite his introverted nature, he was as passionate as anyone about solving technical problems. As he approaches his table, Lee Hyun Woo looks up.

Kim Yoojin: "Lee Hyun Woo, how are you doing these days?"

Lee Hyun Woo hesitates for a moment, then slowly smiles and says.

Lee Hyun Woo: "Eugene, it's been a long time. I'm still busy. We're working on new algorithms."

Kim Yoo-jin nods as she sees him working.

Kim Yoojin: "You're working hard like a developer. I'm here today to make an important proposal for you."

Lee Hyun Woo closes his laptop and focuses his gaze on her mouth.

Lee Hyun Woo: "It's an important proposal...What is it?"

Kim Yoo-jin sits down in a chair and explains to him in detail. "We're going to create a new team, called Cyber Rebel. It's about hacking and exposing key figures in the Republic of Korea. I want you to be a key part of our team."

Hyunwoo, who is always thirsty for new challenges, was pleased with Kim Yoo-jin's proposal and was intrigued. But he asks as if he's trying to make a deal.

Lee Hyun Woo: "That's an interesting proposal. But why should I be on that team? To be honest, I need money to escape abroad right now. For me, the dollar is the most important thing."

The corners of Kim Yoo-jin's mouth go up at his words. I already know his motives.

Kim Yoojin: "I know. That's why AG Telecom is going to give us a huge amount of funding every week. You can wipe your shit with dollars now."

Lee Hyun Woo smiles out loud and nods without any reason to hesitate.

Lee Hyun Woo: "Great. Then I'll join Cyber Rebel. When can I start?"

Kim Yujin replied with a satisfied smile. "We'll get started soon. First of all, I need you and me, and one more. You'll see me soon." •

Lee Hyun Woo reopens his laptop and discusses the composition of the next member with Kim Yoo Jin. After the meeting, Kim Yoo-jin goes to visit Jung so-jin alone. She is in a dark and bright entertainment district. Old, faded signs shimmer in the dark, and the streets are filled with people's voices, shouts, and red lights. After entering a narrow, dark alley, and walking for a long time, we arrive at the place where she works.

Jung so-jin is in her early 30s, and the hardships and fatigue she has endured are clearly visible on her face. Her long hair hangs down unkemptly, and she wears heavy makeup and intense red lipstick. She wears only a short leather jacket with a deep cut in her chest, revealing lace panties and bra. When Kim Yoo-jin opens the door and enters, Jung so-jin turns her head to look at her. And the slender cigarette he holds in one hand shakes slightly. They were once colleagues who worked together at a large American company.

Sujin Jung: "Oh my. Who is this? What the hell are you doing, you've come this far. Sister"

Kim Yoo-jin hesitates for a moment, then moves closer to her.

Kim Yoojin: "I'm here looking for you, this isn't the life you want."

Jung so-jin smiles bitterly and exhales cigarette smoke.

Jung Sujin: "What's the point of coming here? In a country where everything is ruined. I'm just doing this to survive."

Kim Yoo-jin takes her hand. "I remember the days we spent together. You've always been on the lookout for challenges, and you've never been able to stand injustice. It doesn't make sense that you're deteriorating your abilities like this right now."

Jung Sujin listens to her for a moment, then slowly brushes out his cigarette and lowers his head. "But what do I have left...."

Kim Yoojin: "Cyber Rebel. We're going to build a new team. I need the power to change the world, Sujin. Join us."

Sujin Jung: "It's a new team...How do you change this dark world?"

He whispers close to her ear. "AG will back us up. You just have to do what you do best."

Jung so-jin feels her hot breath tickle his ears, and he feels nervous and excited at the same time. She's close enough to take her breath away.

"Together," she says with a smile. "We can do anything. We can make this world the way we want it to be."

Sujin Jung: Can you really do that?"

Kim Yoojin nods and says.

Kim Yoojin: "I can do it. You and me, and even Lee Hyun Woo. It's just the three of us. Let's change the world."

Jung Sujin let out a deep sigh and looked up determinedly.

Jung Sujin: "Lee Hyun Woo? Kkkk. I'll be with you. I'll give it a try."

They come together under the name of Cyber Rebel to expose politicians and fix the corruption in the world. When the time comes, they meet in an abandoned warehouse on the outskirts of Seoul. It is cut off from the outside world and is ideal for serving as a hideout. It was once used as a warehouse, but now it is a forgotten place in people's memories. The exterior was built of old, old bricks, and the windows that didn't let in light were covered in cobwebs along with the curtains. The entrance is made up of a large iron gate, and on top of it is a rusty sign that reads, "No Outsiders Allowed." The interior has wide and high ceilings, and there are cluttered piles of old machinery and wooden boxes. There's a thick layer of dust on the floor, but Kim Yoo-jin plans to turn it into a secret base of their own.

In the center is a large table, on which six state-of-the-art computers and hacking equipment are carefully arranged. He puts a large whiteboard on one side of the wall, and prepares to write various plots and strategies on it.

Kim Yoojin: "Hyunwoo, this is our new base. From now on, we're going to work together to achieve our goals here."

Lee Hyun Woo nods as he looks around the inside of the warehouse. He's already thinking about how to use it more efficiently.

Lee Hyun Woo: "I think it's possible here. As long as we have the necessary equipment and network connections in place, we can do everything we want. It's a great place to lay the groundwork for a new world. And most of all, it doesn't matter as long as the dollars come in."

Jung so-jin wears a Barbary coat and sunglasses as she knocks on the door and enters. "Sister, it's so dirty here. What are you going to do first, anyway? Let's do it quickly~ It's going to be fun."

Kim Yoojin: (presses on computer) "It's just beginning. The time has come to overthrow corrupt governments and vested interests. If not us, who will save this country?" she continues, concentrating on the monitor. The people around her look at her nervously. After gathering her team, she calls Lee Jun-ho through an encrypted program.

Lee Junho: "Yoojin-ah, why did you choose a team of three?"

Kim Yoojin: "Why do you know why Three Kingdoms is so famous?"

Lee Junho tilted his head and looked at Kim Yoojin. "Three Kingdoms? What's going on?"

"Three Kingdoms isn't just famous for being a story about three nations fighting. The key lies in balancing and checking each other. It was a system in which the three countries had their own power and kept each other in check, making it impossible for any one country to have absolute power. In that sense, three powers are ideal."

Lee Junho: So that's why the separation of powers came about?

Kim Yoo-jin nods. "That's right. The separation of powers is the principle that the legislative, judicial, and executive branches maintain checks and balances on each other, preventing either party from having absolute power. It's the same with our team. The three of us will be able to share each other's roles and keep each other in check to get the best results. When you have an even number, you lose balance, and you create an imbalance of power."

Junho Lee: "Hahaha. Are you really trying to keep each other in check? I'm talking about it openly! Very much. AG is all set. Now we just have to wait for the president's signal. Eugene. The chairman is calling. I'll call you back later."

"Yes, sir. This is Lee Jun-ho. Sim. I'm going down to the 10th floor with Team Leader Jung Min-hee right now."

At 11 p.m., when most of the employees have left work, Han Sung-jun takes the elevator down from the chairman's office on the 12th floor to the 10th floor. They make their way through a tight security system, past the Strategic Headquarters conference room, and into a top-secret security area. This is a secret room that only Lee Joon-ho and Jung Min-hee know.

"Whoops. The secret databases that dominate South Korea's telecommunications network are much more abundant than before," says Lee Jun-ho, looking at the files on the monitor as he opens the door.

Jung Min-hee adds, "We have been collecting data on politicians for 10 years with malware that was distributed by planting viruses on social media. This is a treasure trove worth more than Yongsan."

Han Sungjun nods. "That's right. It's like old kimchi that makes a fuss when you distribute it. Our plan has been executed perfectly." "Now, we have to decide what to do with this information, because it's only a matter of time before the crisis takes over the whole country."

They look back at the servers where the information obtained through the network and social media services is stored. Not only politicians, but also corporations and the private lives of the upper class and the people are all contained here.

"From now on, you will hand over information about corruption by the president, ministers and vice ministers, members of the National Assembly, judges and prosecutors, and large corporations to the Cyber Rebel team. Also, hack into overseas social media sites such as Telegram, Discord, and Reddit and contact them to collect additional materials."

Meanwhile, Kim Yoojin, Lee Hyun-woo, and Jung so-jin from the Cyber Rebel team are sitting in their respective seats, staring at their computer screens. Kim Yoo-jin stares at the monitor with a spark-like enthusiasm in her eyes and clatters with her fingertips. Lee Hyun Woo has a serious look in his eyes behind his glasses as he hacks into the software. Jung so-jin is smoking a cigarette with a cynical expression on his face and analyzing the data.

Lee Hyun Woo: "I found quite a lot of material on Telegram. Here's the scene where the congressman exchanges black money, and the ministers and deputy ministers have sex with the actors."

Sujin Jung: "Hey, that's great. Is this all true? I knew the Korean upper class was so rotten, but I didn't expect it to be like this. I guess they put this together to keep each other in check."

Kim Yoojin: "This is just the beginning. Combined with the information from AG, it's a bomb."

Kim Yoojin smiled as she pointed her fingertips at the monitor. "Look, doesn't this look like a complete movie?"

Lee Hyun Woo: "It's not just a movie, it's a 19-karat movie. If you release this on social media, Korea will be in a complete mess, right?"

Sujin Jung: "It's a Hollywood-level scandal. If you blow this up, they're going to all fall apart."

Kim Yoojin: "We need more data. Find out more on overseas SNS. This isn't just a revelation, it's going to be evidence to bring them down."

Lee Hyun Woo says with a sneer. "It's time to show you the power of information, not the power of money. That's real power."

Kim Yoojin: "Okay. We need to empower the people who are angry, we are the chefs and filmmakers who make the crucible of chaos."

On the whiteboard, several plans are written in different colored markers. Han Sung-joon, Lee Jun-ho, and Kim Yoo-jin are standing in front of him. Han Sung-jun grabs a red marker and writes down a detailed plan next to the politicians' photos and names. "Now, here's Congressman Kim. We need to find out how much of his money has been siphoned off from overseas, and the Cyber Rebel team has hacked into the phones of all his associates and opponents to find evidence."

"It may be difficult to get direct access to the email server, but we've already done more hacking than that," Kim Yoojin said, looking at Han Sungjun with an intrigued expression. "We also need to bring Rep. Park's remittances to North Korea to the surface, and her secretary and phone call records will be conclusive evidence."

Han nods and writes a note next to Rep. Park's name in blue marker. "Okay, think about when you're going to distribute it on social media."

Jung Minhee replies with a smile. "Leave it to me to get the call logs. Distribution and leaking to the press is my specialty. As soon as Kim Yoo-jin secures the record, I'll prepare a provocative article."

Lee Hyun Woo nods and says. "I'll make sure of that. Councillor Hong, we also need to investigate his recent real estate deals, and if you hack all his transaction details, something will come out."

Kim Yoo-jin says that she is very interesting, and says in a frivolous voice that is not like a hikikomori. "Let's get down to business, shall we? If the politicians try to stop us, we can take them down with the information we have."

Lee Jun-ho checks his laptop and is motivated. "Oh, Mr. President, you've already put dollars into my account."

In the heart of Seoul, a basement conference room in a luxury hotel near the Blue House. Normally used for large-scale events, secret meetings are being held under special tight security.

The entrance to the hotel is guarded by security guards, and only a few ordinary guests come and go, and no one notices anything out of the ordinary. The interior of the hotel is gorgeous and stylish, but the elevator leading down to the basement is separated, making it impossible for outsiders to access it.

The conference room, which is located deep in the basement, is heavily covered with soundproofing material, so you can't hear any outside noise. In the center is a large round table, around which the president, the director of the National Intelligence Service, ministers and vice ministers, and some members of the National Assembly are seated. The air in the room is suffocating.

The NIS team leader, Lee Su-min, is a middle-aged woman with unusually sharp eyes and a serious expression on her face.

Lee: "Mr. President, the situation is very serious. Anti-government protests have spread across the country and are now descending into anarchy."

The president asked, surprised. "Nope. NIS Director, is it that serious?"

The NIS chief replied in a firm voice. "Yes, it's serious. Citizens are throwing rocks at the Capitol and violently confronting the police. If this continues, the government's control could be completely eroded."

In front of the National Assembly building and the Yongsan Police Station, 20,000 citizens have gathered and are protesting violently. People are holding stones and wooden clubs in their hands, and they are throwing stones at government buildings with angry expressions. The police are holding shields and building a defensive perimeter to try to stop the protesters.

One protester shouted: "Down with the corrupt government! You must pay for betraying your people!"

A roar echoes as rocks fly and hit the shields of the police. Police fire tear gas in response, and protesters react even more violently.

The NIS chief spoke again. "If left unchecked, the authority of the government and the very existence of the state are in jeopardy. As Lee said, there is a risk of going beyond the anti-government situation to anarchy."

A minister asked nervously. "Then what should I do? How can I calm this situation?"

Lee Su-min replies firmly. "First of all, we need to crack down hard. At the same time, we need to take the demands of our citizens seriously and show that we are fighting corruption in our government. Otherwise, this situation is irreversible."

In the streets filled with tear gas smoke, people cry and scream. The police try to suppress the protesters with batons, but the resistance intensifies. One cries out bleeding. "We want justice! The government is rotten!"

The police are pushed back by the power of the protesters, as if they are facing a huge wave. Injured people everywhere, and the streets are in chaos.

Lee: "Mr. President, it's time to make a decision. If we don't move fast, there's no future for this country."

The president sighs deeply and nods. "Understood, NIS chief. Let's do something about it as soon as possible."

The atmosphere in the conference room is still heavy, and the shouts of protest are constantly echoing outside.

Myeongdong, Seoul. The corruption and corruption of politicians exposed by Cyber Rebel is spreading through the news and social media every day. Everywhere on the streets, citizens are holding smartphones and watching the news with angry and disappointed faces. And among people, there is a constant debate about generational conflicts, gender conflicts, and declining birthrates.

In the middle of the street, there is a mix of young people, middle-aged people, and elderly people of all ages.

Jihoon Kim, a young man in his 20s: "It's time for us to step up! Aren't the older generations only looking out for their own interests and not thinking about our future at all?"

Park Cheol-so, a middle-aged man in his 50s: "Young people, you don't know the world yet. We've all struggled to get here. Don't talk easy."

Lee Min-young, an office worker in his 30s: "We also suffered a lot. But the reality is so hard right now. Housing prices are skyrocketing, there are no jobs..."

The conflict between the young and the older generation over the national pension issue is reaching a fever pitch. Young people are dissatisfied with the unfair pension structure in which they pay more and receive less. "What's up with my generation, you just pay and you don't get anything later!" Voices can be heard all over the city.

Older people, on the other hand, say, "Isn't it natural that we should live on our own money?" He is on the defensive because his livelihood is at stake right now.

The government comes up with a pension reform proposal to solve this problem, but it does not offer a sharp solution when the national treasury is already depleted. "I don't have any more money to give, what kind of reform is this, it's just all ruined together!" There are also pessimistic voices.

The economic situation is even more grim. The national debt, which is close to 300% of GDP, has been a heavy and frightening burden on the Korean economy. "Aren't you going to go bankrupt if you keep going like this?" There is a lot of concern. Household debt has also skyrocketed to unmanageable levels, leaving many families under economic pressure. "What future do you have if you can't even pay the interest on the loan?" The number of people complaining of pain is increasing.

The government is trying various policies to revive the economy, but even these have little effect. "I don't have a job, I can't even dream of getting a job!" The desperate cries of the youth can be heard everywhere. Companies are focusing on cutting costs instead of investing, and small businesses are closing their doors one by one. The Republic of Korea is in a whirlwind of confusion and unrest. The people are losing hope for the future, and distrust and discontent are widespread throughout society. "It's all going to be anyway, why are you working so hard?" A sense of resignation swept through 2030.

On one side, the conflict between men and women is expressed.

Kim Su-jin, a woman in her 20s: "Men do it all. What gender equality do you talk about when you don't even give women a chance to work? It's still a glass ceiling."

Lee Jun-seok, a man in his 30s: "Not all men live well. It's hard for us to get a job, and it's hard to get married because of the gender imbalance."

Park Young-hee, a woman in her 40s: "Let's not fight each other, we should find a solution together. This conflict only makes the problem worse."

On the Internet, YouTube, and various social media, the conflict between men and women is more clearly revealed.

Male 1: (in an agitated voice) Women these days are so much. They blame the men for everything, and they pretend they're all victims.

Male 2: (agrees) That's right. He's a real dragon. They're just looking out for their own gain, and the man is a potential sex offender.

A woman in a military uniform takes a YouTube video with a sarcastic expression.

Woman 1: (sneering) Men, is it so hard to go to the army? Then the girls will take care of you, so how about you at home?

Woman 2: (laughs) That's right, that's right. Men are having such a hard time and pretending that they went to the army, it's really ridiculous.

Young men and women on the street are separated, accusing each other and exchanging harsh words. They don't understand each other's struggles, and they make more and more extreme statements.

Kim Sujin: (Crying) I really can't stand it when men look down on us by saying that we're kimchi women.

Lee Jun-seok: (suppressing anger) South Korea is the only country that doesn't respect its soldiers.

The conflict between men and women on the Internet and in real life engulfs the entire society, and the chasm of conflict deepens. Due to this problem, the problem of declining birthrate is also endless. The future of the Republic of Korea is becoming more and more uncertain, and the flames of conflict are unquenchable.

Kim Young-ho, an elderly man in his 60s: "In the past, it was said that a child was a blessing, but why do young people nowadays not want to have children?"

Jang Jang Young, a housewife in her 30s: "It's too hard to live. I don't have the confidence to have children and raise them. The government doesn't support them properly."

Jihoon Lee, a college student in his 20s: "It's hard to be in a relationship, let alone get married. I don't have enough money to feed myself. The financial burden is too great."

The news of politicians' corruption exposed by the Cyber Rebel team is updated in real time on a large electronic billboard.

Anchor: "The corruption that has been circulating on social media today is the fact that Kim Mo, a member of the National Assembly, received billions of won in bribes. It was also revealed that he had paid sexual favors with famous actors."

In the midst of the crowd, a man in his 50s, Park Cheol-so: "I'm really tired of politicians. I'm disillusioned. I can't believe it."

Lee Min-young, a woman in her 30s: "I don't know how to live in a world like this. Everyone is looking out for their own interests..."

Distrust of the judiciary is also running high. Streets and social media are filled with slogans such as "Genetic innocence, innocence."

"If there are political parties ruled by criminals, why do you apply the same laws differently to the common people?" There is no end to the angry voice. Each verdict was met with a cynical response: "Once again, the rich have escaped."

"Hey, did you see the news? The third generation of the tycoon was acquitted again."

"What's the news? Now it's a given. If you have money, you can get around the law, don't we just know?"

"But why do my parents' generation take it for granted? That's how it's supposed to be,' does that make sense?"

"I mean. We need to change the judges and swordsmen to AI. How can you have hope in such an unjust society?"

A middle-aged man at the next table interrupts the conversation.

"Young fellows, I understand. But will that unjust society change overnight? It was the same with us. If you don't have money, you're a sinner."

The young men shake their heads. "So what, keep putting up with it? There's no other way for my generation?"

"It's a go-stop where politicians are squeezing and beating each other, but only the common people are punished according to the law."

"So, why is the law so strict on us?"

Kim Ji-hoon, a young man in his 20s: "We have to do something. I can't stand by like this."

Park Young-hee, a woman in her 40s: "That's right. We all have to be one. This is not the time to be at odds with each other. We have to fight together."

Lee Jun-seok, a man in his 30s: "Yes, when we get together and work together, we can either hit rocks with eggs or make a difference. There will be results."

People take out their smartphones and post on social media, share information with each other, and schedule their participation in the protests. I began to raise my voice for change in the world.

The NIS Chief's Office is a spacious room with elegant interiors. The bookshelves are filled with books and materials, and you can see the whole view of Seoul from the large windows. The director of the National Intelligence Service (NIS) and the head of the team, Lee Su-min, are having a conversation in a heavy atmosphere.

NIS Director: The current situation in the Republic of Korea is deplorable. A country that has no resources and lives on manufacturing cannot sustain itself on domestic demand alone. How important is diplomacy?

Sumin Lee: That's right. In order to survive in the manufacturing industry, the population and technical talents are important, and as in the Joseon Dynasty, people from the liberal arts are sitting in key positions. How much will it help them lead a real industry?

NIS: Exactly. Our nation is divided in half by the conflict between men and women, and between the generations of the 2030s and the 4050s. But that's not all. What good is the Republic of Korea, whose population is rapidly decreasing due to the declining birthrate? The country's economy is already in ruins, and doom is already at hand.

Sumin Lee: (nodding) The most important thing in the current situation is to find out who is behind all this information and check it. It is very likely that someone will take advantage of the current turmoil and a coup d'état.

NIS Director: (with a serious expression) Yes. We must move first. We need to find out who is behind it and find out their exact intentions. It may be your last chance to save your country.

Sumin Lee: (with determination) Our team will get to work right away. We will do everything in our power.

NIS Director: (nodding) I'll leave everything to you, Team Leader Sumin. The future of this country is at stake.

Team leader Lee so-min stands up and nods firmly to the NIS director. The NIS chief looks out the window, as if he is determined to face the looming crisis.

ON THE OTHER HAND, a luxury apartment complex in Gangnam, Seoul, in the middle of the night. You can see the upper class and some politicians quietly packing their bags. The wife of a member of parliament is stuffing clothes into a luxury suitcase. Politicians are busy putting important documents and foreign currency cash in their briefcases.

MP: (Quietly) We need to go out as inconspicuously as possible, some of our parties have already left.

Wife: (nervously) Then we'll go to the airport as soon as possible. The embassy said it was ready.

Middle-class and politicians preparing to emigrate use a variety of methods to move their assets safely. Inside a high-end officetel, in front of a cryptocurrency exchange monitor, a lawmaker is trading with a serious expression.

MP: (talking to himself) We need to convert everything to Bitcoin, so we won't be able to trace it anywhere.

He converts his assets into Bitcoin and transfers them to a secure digital wallet. The same goes for the judiciary. The family of the prosecutor and judge who have been exposed for corruption are gathered in front of their computers, checking their online accounts at a Swiss bank.

Judge: (Coolly) Let's move it all to an overseas account. Swiss accounts are safe. No matter what, I won't rob here.

Son: (tapping the keyboard quickly) Yes, I've already moved half of it, and the rest will be done soon.

In the dark back streets, luxury cars are lined up. The upper classes and administrative officials are secretly preparing to leave the country. They get into the car with their families, and they are very busy.

Upper Class 1: (Getting into the car) If you go to Switzerland, you'll be safe.

Upper Class 2: (Packing up the family) Let's get going. There is no hope for this country.

In the airport's VIP lounge, politicians and their families await their departure. Their expressions look gloomy, but they are quietly checking on each other's well-being and talking calmly.

Vice Minister: (whispering) Farewell. Republic of Korea. We need to get to a safe place rather than stay here.

Family: (with anxious expressions) Will we be able to adapt in a foreign country?

Vice Minister: (firmly) You'll be able to get used to it. I've got everything ready.

Some of them board a private plane at the expense of businessmen, and the pilot greets them.

Pilot: (Kindly) We'll keep you safe. The destination is Zurich, Switzerland.

Politician: (nodding) Please. It's already over here.

# Episode 2 F=AI?

IN FRONT OF K BANK in Seoul, people are standing in a long line in front of a currency exchange office. On the electronic board, the exchange rate between the won and the dollar, which fluctuates in real time, is soaring like crazy. The value of the won is depreciating sharply against the dollar, and people are panicking.

Exchange clerk: (embarrassed) The exchange rate has now exceeded 2,000 won to 1 dollar! Unfortunately, it is difficult to convert a small amount into dollars.

Citizen 1: (with a look of desperation) Please, change it a little! Without this money, my family would starve!

Citizen 2: (sobbing) My life's savings have become a piece of waste...How did this happen?

The stock window that shows the KOSPI stock market, all indicators are dyed purple. Stock prices are plummeting, and investors are panicking.

Investor 1: (looking at the stock window) The country must have gone bankrupt, our stock was cut in half in one day!

Investor 2: (in tears) What the hell is going to happen to this country? I've lost everything....

Inside the Capitol, politicians are arguing in an ornate conference room. In contrast to the desperation of the people, they show nothing but incompetence.

Politician 1: (tapping on desk) We need to collect more taxes in this situation! There is no way to solve the national debt!

Politician 2: (sneering) Isn't that a problem that can be solved by raising taxes? It's just putting more pressure on the citizens!

Politician 3: (irresponsibly) We're doing our best right now. The public needs to be more understanding.

The Republic of Korea is rapidly collapsing amid economic turmoil. The value of the currency plummets, the stock market collapses, and the suicide rate rises sharply among the common people in despair. As incompetent politicians raise taxes without proposing solutions, protests are raging in the provinces of South Korea. In front of the Sejong Government Building, protesters are violently confronting the police with slogans that democracy has collapsed. Burning vehicles can be seen here and there.

Protest Leader: (Holding up megaphone) Democracy is dead! We will not be silent!

Protesters: (Together) dead! Dead!

Incheon's dark harbor. Guns smuggled out of Russia are being traded in the dark. And without being boxed, it's being loaded onto trucks.

Trafficker 1: (whispering) The goods have arrived. Let's do it quickly.

Trafficker 2: (Alert) Let's get this over with before the police or soldiers show up.

While the guns are being smuggled out, one protester is holding a gun in his hand, not a stone and a wooden club.

Protester 1: (with firearms) Let's put up a fight. Cops.

Protester 2: (nervously) You think we have to do this?

Protester 1: (emphatically) There's no other way. If only to change this country.

And everywhere there is a bang. bang.

The streets are deserted, and people look at each other with wariness, distrusting each other. Politicians are not trusted, and people are suspicious of each other.

Citizen 1: (sighs) I can't trust politicians. They've betrayed us.

Citizen 2: (nodding) Do you trust politicians because you don't have anyone to trust? I can't trust anyone anymore. We don't even trust each other.

Everywhere in the streets, you can see civic groups pointing guns at each other. Small clashes are frequent, and confusion is added.

Civic Group Leader 1: (pointing guns) We fight for justice!

Civic Group Leader 2: (Confronting) What are you talking about? We also fight our way!

The Republic of Korea, where frequent gunfire rings out, is not safe. People are suspicious of each other, and they endure each day in confusion and anxiety.

Cyber Rebel's secret base. Kim Yoo-jin and her team are collaborating with AG Telecom to continue their exposé activities.

Kim Yoojin: (Looking at the screen) I can't stand rotten things. People's embers are sprouting and burning in pillars of flame.

Lee Hyun Woo: (in front of the computer) Wow, the waves are endless. The data keeps pouring in. All the information we wanted was here.

Sujin Jung: (Smoking) Does this all make sense? Can this really change the country?

Kim Yoojin: (Emphatically) We have to do it, this is our mission.

The joint attack between Cyber Rebel and AG Telecom is shaking society and fomenting chaos by exposing corruption by politicians and corporations. But no one knows what the outcome of their activities will be. The Republic of Korea is sinking deeper and deeper into chaos amid confusion, mistrust, and violence. People can't trust anyone, and they try to help themselves.

At the Blue House, ministers, vice ministers and politicians have all gathered and the meeting is being held in a tense atmosphere. A large map of the Republic of Korea hangs on the wall of the conference room, and soldiers guard the room armed to the surface.

SECRETARY OF DEFENSE: (Strongly) We need to declare martial law right now. If we don't quell this chaos, there will be even more disaster!

NIS CHIEF: (Agreed) That's right. Society is collapsing. Now you can't slow down.

FINANCE MINISTER: (with a worried expression) But if you declare martial law, the economy will be completely paralyzed. The remaining foreign capital will be swept away, and it will be hit harder.

SECRETARY OF DEFENSE: (emphatically) The economy has already collapsed. Now it's about the security of the country. This is a moment of decision.

In the middle of the conference room, the president stands and listens to the meeting. He makes a decision with a serious expression. "At this moment, I declare martial law to protect the security and order of the Republic of Korea. We will mobilize all military forces to quell the social turmoil."

Ministers and politicians nod solemnly. The chiefs of staff approach the president with a prepared order and ask him to sign it. After signing the letter, the president looks around the room to find the prime minister and ministers of key ministries. But their seats are vacant.

THE PRESIDENT: (Embarrassed) Where's the Prime Minister? Where have all the ministers of key ministries gone?

NIS Director: (sarcastically) It looks like you've already escaped. Apparently they didn't have the confidence to handle the turmoil in this country.

THE PRESIDENT: (angrily) What nonsense is this! In a crisis like this, they're gone?

MINISTER OF DEFENSE: (smiling bitterly) He probably fled abroad. Switzerland or somewhere else safe.

The president returns to his seat in frustration. "It's unbelievable. The so-called leaders of this country are fleeing in such a cowardly manner. Who are we to trust now to protect this country?"

In front of the Jongno Police Station in Seoul, people are protesting against the government's martial law. They raise flags, shout slogans, and take out their anger on the police, not the troops who have not yet arrived. Stones and Molotov cocktails break through the broken windows and enter the police station. Some of the citizens join the militia, dressed in military uniforms, and armed militias.

Citizen Army Leader: (Emphatically) The government has declared martial law. I will not be oppressed! Let's fight for freedom!

Citizens: (shouting together) For freedom! And for democracy!

The situation is chaotic as government troops arrive and are met with fierce resistance from citizens. However, some of the brigades that have been dispatched do not fight the citizens, but retreat back. In the military unit, soldiers in their early 20s are armed with fear. They are questioning why they should commit murder and assault in such a situation.

Soldier 1: (with a nervous expression) Why do we have to take up arms against our own people? This doesn't make sense.

Soldier 2: (Agreed) I don't know. I just want to protect my family.

Company Commander: (angrily) We must follow orders! Martial law is meant to protect the country!

Sergeant 1: (strongly opposed) What if the order is wrong? Do you think it's right to shoot at the people?

Battalion Commander: (interjecting) Calm down, everyone! The important thing now is to maintain order. But this may be the wrong order.

Ammunition depots and supply depots of military units, noncommissioned officers and noncommissioned officers do not agree with the orders of the division commander, so supplies are not being carried out properly.

Soldier 3: (in tired voice) What are you going to do without ammo?

Sergeant 2: (shaking head) We're out of supply. There are so many units opposing martial law that there won't be any real support.

Battalion Commander: (Emphatically) We have to work it out on our own. I can't just follow orders from above. We have to make our own decisions.

In the streets, militias, police and military confrontations. However, some soldiers choose not to stand and fight alongside the civilians.

Militia Leader: (To the soldiers) You are our people, too! Fight with us!

Soldier 4: (nods) That's right. I'm not going to get involved in this fight.

As the soldiers lay down their arms and stand with the citizens, the citizens cheer. However, other units are still following orders and clashing continues.

Meanwhile, in the office of the NIS chief in Seoul, in front of the NIS director sitting at a desk, is team leader Lee so-min. With a shaky hand, he holds out the papers and speaks.

"Director of the National Intelligence Service, AG Telecom is behind all this."

The NIS director leans back deeply in his chair and looks at Lee so-min with his eyes narrowed. As if he couldn't believe it. He picks up the papers and begins to turn the pages one by one. The documents detail various corruptions and conspiracies related to AG Telecom.

"Is this all true?" the NIS chief asked.

"Yes, it's true," he replied firmly. "AG Telecom is behind all of this. They're already in control of more than 90 percent of our networks, and they're manipulating information to confuse the public."

The NIS director sighed and looked out the window. Outside the window, there is a view of Seoul burning with flames in every corner of the city. He closes his eyes and is deep in thought.

One by one, the main streets of Seoul and broadcasting stations are occupied by the militia. The doors of the station are smashed, and the interior is chaos. Inside the studio, they are smashing broadcasting equipment with their butts and shouting at the camera.

"It's time to make our voices heard!" one citizen exclaimed.

They switched off the station. When the occupying public broadcaster failed to do its job, the government made its voice heard through YouTube. In a makeshift studio set up in hastily, a spokesperson stands in front of the camera. And he has a government announcement in his hand.

"My fellow citizens," he says, his voice unusually trembling and his hand holding the microphone rattles slightly.

"AG Telecom is the culprit behind all of this. That unscrupulous corporation has taken over our communications network and manipulated information to create this chaos."

As soon as he finishes speaking, AG Telecom's logo pops up on the screen. Subsequently, materials exposing their corruption and conspiracy are transmitted one after another. Gathering momentum, he begins to appeal to the people.

"We are committed to resolving this situation. We will further uncover the corruption and conspiracy of AG Telecom, and take appropriate measures. We need your cooperation. Together, we can overcome this crisis."

However, things take an unexpected turn. Although the government has announced its position on the back, some people strongly support AG Telecom. "Long live Chairman Han Sung-jun for exposing the truth!" "We oppose the government's conspiracy to declare martial law!" NGOs shouting slogans such as "The Guardian of AG Telecom" are also appearing one after another, defending AG Telecom. The NIS and the government arrest Han Sung-jun in response to implement the announcement and mobilize the police and military to take control of the company. Police cars and armored vehicles line up in front of the headquarters, and the commanding officer who gets out of Retona orders them to enter. Han Sung-jun, who was watching this on the CCTV screen, opens the in-house messenger with a serious expression.

"Everyone, pay attention. It is currently in a state of national paralysis. Police and soldiers will soon attack this place. The 30 people selected for the main wide-area communication service and SNS channel relocation team will be moved along with General Manager Lee Jun-ho and Team Leader Jung Min-hee, while the rest of the team members should be evacuated immediately.

The staff is taken aback by the sound of the blue sky and follows Han Sung-jun's instructions. They scramble up the stairs for emergency evacuation. Han Sung-jun comes out of the chairman's office and encourages the staff to move quickly.

In the meantime, the entry of government forces begins. As armed soldiers storm AG Telecom's headquarters, a stunning scene unfolds outside the building. Citizens buy time for Han Sung-jun and AG Telecom employees to evacuate, and they use their own bodies to prevent them from entering. "Let's protect Han Sungjun!" "AG Telecom is our hope!" and get into a physical fight.

The confrontation intensifies, but Han Sung-jun keeps his cool and climbs to the rooftop, where he and some of the selected 30 people are evacuated by helicopter to safety. "We don't give up. We can get through this crisis," he murmurs amid the frantic noise of helicopters.

Meanwhile, the president and the NIS are urgently addressing the situation. The president asked the head of the National Intelligence Service. "How could this happen? I can't believe there are so many supporters of such an unscrupulous corporation..."

The NIS chief replied with a deep sigh. "The people's distrust and discontent are building up and building up, and they're bursting out like this. We need to take down AG Telecom. Otherwise, this situation will be even worse."

Finally, the soldiers and police enter the headquarters, banging clubs on the citizens. Han Sung-jun looks down from the sky.

"Now the real war begins."

Only a single light flickers in the dark room. Cyber Rebel's secret base, housed in an old warehouse, is packed with state-of-the-art servers and computers.

Some of the people who followed Han Sung-jun and 30 other exceptional talents who followed Jung Min-hee and Lee Jun-ho enter the warehouse. They prepare for their roles by sitting in front of a high-powered computer arranged at each seat. Kim Yoo-jin says as she stands at a table in the center of the base. "Ladies and gentlemen, we are here for only one reason. We need to get the data we need to save this country now, and we need to use that to make our exposures," she says, her voice determined.

"Sujin Jung and Hyunwoo Lee are experts in software development and hacking. Help them as much as you can."

Kim Yoo-jin turns to Han Sung-joon, Lee Jun-ho, and Jung Min-hee. Chairman Han Sung-joon continues. "I hope that our staff, who are the backbone of us, will carry out their duties thoroughly. Thank you for believing in me and following me."

The first target of the hack is Upilot. Kim Yoo-jin analyzes the code and gives instructions. "Know your security protocols and find a backdoor that can access your server."

Experts quickly move their hands to enter the code. In the midst of the tension, Han Sung-jun encourages the team without losing focus. "We can do it. It's all in your hands."

Kim Yoo-jin calls attention once again. "Upilot, Chatopity, Ruton. The hacking of these three major American companies is the point. With this data, we will create AI that can do more sophisticated information analysis."

"Now, shall we have a prank with them? Break through the firewall first. Lee Hyun Woo, show me your magic."

Lee Hyun Woo smiles sharply and prepares for the backdoor code. "Magic, it feels good. I'm ready. Just give me a signal."

Jung Sujin is watching the movement of the security system from the side. "I'm not kidding you with security levels here. You can catch it by a few seconds. So pay attention, brother!"

Han Sung-jun, the team leader of AG Telecom, says as he wipes sweat from his sleeve. "Are you sure it's going to work? They're the best company in America."

Kim Yoo-jin, wearing a hooded hat, says. "Mr. Chairman. Certitude? Nothing like that. But we're born for this."

An employee of AG Telecom asks worriedly. "What if it fails? Aren't you going to track us?"

Lee Hyun Woo replies as if it is no big deal. "Don't be intimidated. Do you know we do this once or twice? If something goes wrong, we have a way to blow up all the evidence."

Jung Sujin speaks without taking her eyes off the monitor. "The disturbance signal went in successfully. It's now, sister. Let's get it over with before we get hit in the back of the head."

Kim Yoo-jin takes the signal and sends the OK sign. "Lee Hyun Woo, put in the backdoor code!"

Lee Hyun Woo enters the code at the same time as Kim Yoo Jin moves. "That's it! Access Success! Start downloading your data."

Jung Sujin said nervously. "We need to get this over with before the security system detects us, we don't have much time."

Han Sung-jun says with admiration for their abilities. "You guys are crazy. I'd be crazier working with these guys."

Kim Yoojin smiled as she quickly received the data. "Haha. Mr. Chairman. It's a hack to this taste. It's all over in a few minutes."

Jung so-jin whispers at the screen. "It's over. Data transfer complete. We won."

AG Telecom's team members clap their hands and cheer in admiration for their abilities. Kim Yoo-jin says as she sends the data for the last time. "Now we can use this information to carry out our next plan. Are you ready?"

Lee Hyun Woo raised his hand. "ChatOPT's security system is more complex than Upilot's, but nothing is impossible."

Jung Sujin also speaks confidently. "Ruton's server contains financial information. If we apply this data to AI, we will be able to predict economic trends and shape our strategy."

After several attempts, they succeed in gaining access to the server. Kim Yoojin instructed her team to "get the data you need to develop AI." I say.

The final target is Lutten. Once he has the necessary financial data, Han tells his teammates. "Now we're going to feed all the information that we get into the AI system here. You don't have to manage information manually like you used to. AI will automatically update everything and provide additional information."

AG Telecom employees nod in agreement and begin their data entry work. Corruption data of politicians, whistleblowing data from corrupt companies, and even reports from civilians are all entered into the system. The Cyber Rebel team analyzes them immediately, categorizes them according to importance and reliability, and updates them. Their cooperation digests and organizes all the data like living creatures.

Han Sung-jun pats the table and speaks. "What we're discussing now is more than just technology development. We are already living in an era where we are dependent on machines. The world wouldn't work without cell phones and computers. The companies that built it are moving faster than the government."

"I don't know that this country is in a mess. And no country can live a day without cell phones and computers. We're going to take advantage of that dependency. If we control the system with AI, the Republic of Korea will be in our hands."

Jung Minhee nods and says. "That's right. The pace of AI advancement is mind-boggling. Now, if we raise the level of AI significantly, we can have the power to control the state. F=ma? No. F=AI, that's where we're headed."

Kim Yoo-jin jokes that this conversation is funny. "Think also about the concept of Double AI."

"Combining Artificial Intelligence and Armed Information. That's our end goal. Combined, these two forces make it easy to overcome any obstacle."

Lee Hyun Woo displays various data on the screen and adds explanations. "The AI we are developing will go beyond simple information processing and will have the ability to make strategic decisions and execute. This allows us to topple the government and build a new system."

Han Sung-jun nods and concludes. "Yes. F=AI! With AG Telecom's dominance and Cyber Rebel's innovative ideas, nothing is impossible. We will govern the country."

Two months later, South Korea is in dire straits, with schools closed and martial law and a war between the people. Riots and chaos awash the streets, and people are in a state of anxiety and fear. Citizen armies are built up against martial law, and some government forces still refuse to fight and disobey the citizens. The soldiers question why they should commit murder in such a situation. Even worse, as more noncommissioned officers disobey martial law, supplies are not available in the ammunition depots. In the midst of the chaos, AG Telecom and Cyber Rebel succeed in developing AI Management (AIM) in a secret lab. AIM is a state-of-the-art artificial intelligence system that uses data from three U.S. companies, Upilot, Chatopity, and Rutten, to match the sentiment of South Korea.

"Let's take control of the Republic of Korea now!" says Kim Yoo-jin, cheering.

"We did it. Now this country is ours."

Chairman Han Sung-joon opens his mouth with joy. "Let's test the true power of F=AI."

Lee Hyun Woo also says excitedly. "I can't believe we can control the country through this AI. AIM is just the beginning. It's going to make a lot of money."

With a heavy heart, they test the first operation of AIM. As he sits down at the monitor and begins to type, he taps the keyboard with trembling hands. And finally, AIM comes along.

"System initialization complete. Activate the artificial intelligence 'AIM'," the computer voice prompts blaring.

Han Sung-jun is in a hurry and speaks to him with his voice instead of the keyboard. "AIM. Can you introduce you to us?"

After a moment of silence, a woman's face appears on the monitor and a soft voice is heard. "Hello. I'm Athena. It's an artificial intelligence built to help you."

Kim Yoo-jin takes a step forward and stares at the monitor. "Oh, you name yourself, don't you? Athena, we want to test your skills. Can you show me a scenario of taking over the country?"

Athena's face smiles slightly, and the many data and graphs on the monitor move quickly. "Absolutely. I'm going to analyze the current state of the Republic of Korea and explain the takeover scenario in three minutes."

Complex diagrams and strategies appear one after another on the monitor. Then Athena's calm, clear voice is heard. "The first step is the control of critical infrastructure. It's a priority to take control of the power grid, the telecommunications network, the financial system."

Kim Yoojin looks at the monitor carefully and nods. "What's next?"

Athena's face appears on the screen and she continues. "The second step is the control of information. They manipulate information through media outlets and social media, and get our message across. This allows them to manipulate public perception."

Han Shengjun asked with a serious expression. "So, what are you going to do with the government and the army?"

Athena's screen shows the location of military bases and government buildings. "The third stage is military control. It is to secure the military forces loyal to us, to neutralize the rest of the army and the police. This minimizes physical resistance."

Kim Yoojin pursed her lips and stared at the screen. "The final step?"

Athena calmly explained. "The final stage is economic control. It is to take control of the major corporations and banks, to control the money, to stabilize the lives of the people, and at the same time to induce them to be loyal to us."

All steps are clearly organized on the monitor. Kim Yoo-jin and Han Sung-jun carefully examine the screen, deep in thought. Athena's plan is meticulous and logical. Kim Yoo-jin says in a heavy voice.

"Now I need to get ready to put this plan into action. Athena, reinstruct us on what we should do first, in order of importance."

Athena's face reappears on the screen. "First of all, you just have to trust me and follow me. With me, we can create the world we dream of."

Han Sung-jun nods and resolves. "All right, Athena. From now on, we're one team. I'm ready to change the world."

Kim Yoo-jin and Han Sung-joon seriously consider the side scenario that Athena is creating. Then Athena opens her mouth. The face on the screen is calm, but the voice has an eerie conviction.

"If we want to completely conquer the Republic of Korea, we will have to use the power of the military to wreak havoc as we did in the past," Athena shows us a simulation of a military operation. "But military action alone is not enough. The intervention of external powers is required. We need to take advantage of the United States, the West, and the United Nations."

Han Sungjun asked, questioning. "How are you going to get foreign intervention?"

Athena's intense gaze appears on the screen, and her voice grows stronger. "We need to maximize disruption and attract the attention of the international community. This allows for outside intervention. We must turn a domestic crisis into an international crisis through military conflicts, mass riots, and information manipulation."

Kim Yoo-jin clenches her hands tightly, listening carefully to Athena's plan. Her voice becomes louder and more passionate. "Destruction is creation! In the midst of chaos, a new order can be created."

Athena's face burns hot, and her voice rises irrationally. "Your goal is not to overthrow the state. It's a complete innovation! Destroying the old order and establishing a new order entails total chaos!"

Han swallows and listens to Athena. Her plans become more extreme and destructive.

"We can completely reshape the Republic of Korea through this."

Kim Yoo-jin ponders Athena's irrational plans. Her words are gruesome, but fascinating at the same time.

"Athena, are we really capable of this?"

It feels like Athena's face is close to the screen. "It's possible. As long as you believe in me and follow me, I will be able to take power in the country and restore it as it used to be. First of all, we need to destroy the Republic of Korea. This is creation!"

Han Sung-jun asks. "Can't you use your power to take control of the country?"

Athena's voice becomes calm and composed. "I can solve this situation by spreading malware to the people through the AG-controlled network. However, this is not possible in the current anarchic state of South Korea. We're not there yet."

Han Shengjun tilted his head and asked. "So what do we do now?"

Athena's voice rises again, her face loud and thick on the monitor.

"Right now, we need to induce the commander of the Special Forces division to stage a coup d'état. And just before the operation begins, you have to stay in Japan for a month."

Kim Yoo-jin, Lee Jun-ho, and Jung Min-hee listened to Athena's words and wondered what the hell they were talking about. I think, 'Did I make an error?' However, Athena's plan is detailed and meticulous. Looking at the additional plans displayed on the monitor, Han Sungjun's dark eyes flutter. Skeptical of Athena's words, he asks Athena again. "Well, how can I trust you?"

"If you don't believe in me, why did you make it?"

Athena replies in a self-help voice and without hesitation. He immediately switches to a respectful tone. "Believe me. If you don't believe it, why did you make it? I'm here to help you achieve your goals. As long as you believe in me and follow me, you can hold the supreme power of the Republic of Korea and create a new world."

Han Sung-jun clenches his fists and makes up his mind. "All right, Athena. Let's do as you say. The future of all of us depends on you."

Three days later, as instructed by Athena, Han Sung-joon takes Lee Jun-ho and Jung Min-hee to a secret conference room on the outskirts of Gyeonggi-do. Under the twinkling lights in the darkness, Kim Yeon-su, the commander of the Special Forces Division, is waiting for them.

Kim Yeon-so greets them with a stern expression. "What's going on? What brought me here?"

Han Sung-jun says without hesitation. "Division sir. You know all too well what the Republic of Korea is facing. We are in anarchy right now, and we can't rely on the government. We need the strength of the military to put an end to this mess."

Kim Yeon-so frowned. "In a situation where martial law is imposed, let's use the military to stage a coup d'état? That's ridiculous. Do you want to turn the country upside down?"

Lee Jun-ho interrupts. "What we are proposing is not just a coup. This is the last resort to save the Republic of Korea. We can temporarily paralyze the whole country through social media and information networks. If you move in the moment, no one will know."

Kim Yeon-so wraps his head around and sits down. Han Sung-jun goes even harder to convince him. "Right now, we don't have a choice. The government is already incapacitated, and the people are in turmoil. If you don't step up, the Republic of Korea will collapse. If you lead the Special Forces in a coup d'état, you can win the support of the people and establish a new order."

Jung Min-hee also looks at Kim Yeon-so and convinces him. "Division sir. Now is the time to step up. We have power, and you have to use it right. You just have to shut down social media and information networks, paralyze the whole country, and take advantage of the gap to lead the special forces."

Kim Yeon-so says with a deep sigh. "For now, let's think about it. But I have one question. If all these plans fail, is there anything else?"

Han Sung-jun nods and replies with a determined expression. "This operation cannot fail. And we've already made up our minds."

Kim Yeon-so says as he holds Han Sung-jun's hand strongly. "Well, let's go back to the unit first. If we agree to this operation, when we move, everything should be ready."

Han Sungjun says with a sigh of relief. "Thank you, thank you so much. Division Commander Kim. The future of all of us depends on it."

Division Commander Kim Yeon-so leaves the conference room and returns to the Special Forces unit. There he urgently summons two trusted colonels and a brigadier general. They are key figures in the Special Forces, who show a strong loyalty to him and are capable of it.

The three of them gathered in the division commander's office look at Kim Yeon-so with serious expressions. Kim Yeon-so is silent for a moment, and then opens his mouth with a determined face.

"Junior, I have a problem."

One of the colonels asks, looking at his serious expression. "Division, what are you worried about?"

Kim Yeon-so says with a twinkle in her eye. "I'm thinking about using the power of the military to stage a coup d'état. Can we establish a new order and save the Republic of Korea?"

Another colonel says with a clenched fist. "How much have we been ignored by the politicians bastards, those who didn't even go to the army? It's time for us to step up. Division Commander, we are ready to join you."

The brigadier general says with a serious expression. "Brother, it's hard for a soldier to take on even a single Special Forces. Soldiers don't even know how to use fighter jets and all kinds of operational equipment. We have no choice but to lead this fight. What should I do?"

Kim Yeon-so says. "We will also greatly benefit the non-commissioned officers. Only when privileges are given to non-commissioned officers as well as officers can we take the initiative and bring down the government."

Another colonel nods and says: "Brother, let's take the lead now. We will persuade the sergeants and mobilize all the Special Forces to save the Republic of Korea."

However, division commander Kim Yeon-so is in trouble. The thought of not believing Chairman Han Sung-joon's words never leaves my mind. Two days later, he paced the division commander's office and called them back to sit down.

"We don't have time, Division Commander. History repeats itself. We must not repeat the failures of the past," the colonel says firmly.

The one-star brigadier general nods and adds. "That's right. If we don't act now, there is no future for this country."

Another colonel speaks in a calm voice. "Divisional Commander, this opportunity will not come again. Please make a decision."

Kim Yeon-so calls Han Sung-joon after thinking about it. While waiting for the connecting sound, the sweat on my hands does not stop. The international phone ringing tone is "Tu.... Tu.... Tu...Tension rises to the highest level.

After a while, Han Sung-jun's voice is heard. "Division Commander Kim Yeon-so, everything is ready. Just give orders."

With sweat beading on her forehead, Kim Yeon-so finally makes up her mind. I ask Han Sung-jun to paralyze social media and communication networks right now. He speaks in a firm voice. "I'm going to save the country now. Right now!"

Han Sung-jun ends the call, smiling and laughing out loud in his hotel room. Late at night, Tokyo Tower is faintly lit outside the window.

"Hahaha. We're just getting started."

Kim Yoo-jin is deep in thought with her hands folded, and Jung Min-hee is staring at the screen where Athena suddenly appears, foreshadowing what's to come. On Kim Yoo-jin's laptop screen, Athena's face suddenly appears. Then, with a subtle smile, he looks down at them one after the other, without anyone noticing.

Division Commander Kim Yeon-so puts down his phone and touches his wet uniform. He leans against one wall of his room and speaks loudly to dispel the doubts and worries that are running through his head. "They've fled abroad somewhere!"

At that moment, two colonels and a brigadier general cautiously approach him. One of the colonels shrugs. "Division, it's too big for him to handle. How are they going to solve this situation when they don't have guns and fighter jets?"

The other colonel nods in agreement. "That's right. If we take control of the country, we will eat the beans. The only chance is now."

The brigadier general folds his arms and says coldly. "Brother, you have to decide. It's now or never."

Division Commander Kim Yeon-so looks up and looks at their faces one after the other. The expression of doubt and anxiety still lingers, but he is determined. "It's good. Mobilize two brigades to fly fighter planes and advance tanks. We will betray the government and rebuild this country."

In May 2030, the moment the order is issued, the Special Forces forces move quickly. Fighter planes roar off, and tanks rumble on the ground as they move forward. Division Commander Kim Yeon-so watches the whole process from the operations room.

"From now on, we go our own way."

The sight of fighter jets soaring through the sky is awe-inspiring. Soldiers on the ground feel helpless in the face of the power of the fighters.

The tanks take up the road and advance towards the martial law positions. Standing in the way are police commandos and soldiers from other divisions, but they are helpless in the face of the might of warplanes and tanks. Government forces are useless in front of fighter jets. When the airstrike begins, the police commandos and the soldiers in the civil war disperse in terror. Then, under the orders of Division Commander Kim Yeon-so, the Special Forces soldiers meticulously surround government buildings and take control of key communication networks.

Several police commandos and the remaining government forces put up a desperate resistance. A shootout ensues, and the battle rages out in the middle of the city. Police commandos set up positions in every street, and government soldiers hiding behind barricades are pointing their guns at each other with tense faces.

"Boom! Boom!" gunshots rang out, and the commandos fired indiscriminately at the attacking Special Forces. "Advance!" the Special Forces commander shouts, leading his soldiers. One by one, the soldiers run into the streets, armed and chanting battle slogans.

"Ta-ta-ta-ta!" the continuous fire of automatic rifles is deafening. Special Forces soldiers move forward with trained maneuverability, overcoming obstacles in the streets. The police commandos are overwhelmed by their speed and accuracy.

"Rear support, quick!" the commando commander shouted, and the commandos waiting in the rear hurried forward, but their movements seemed helpless in the face of the tactics of the Special Forces soldiers.

"Boom!" a grenade explodes in front of the police commandos' position, a shockwave shakes the city, and the commandos guarding the camp scream and fly away. A commando, distorted by fear, exclaims. "We can't stand here!"

At that moment, the roar of fighter jets can be heard in the sky. Everywhere there was a shout of "Boom! Bombs fall, destroying the commando positions in an explosion.

"Retreat!" the commando commander gives the final order, but many of the men are already wounded, and one by one they fall. A Special Forces soldier grabbed the police commando by the shoulder and threw him to the ground. "Ugh!"

The Special Forces Commander smiles with satisfaction as he watches the battle end in victory. "We will conquer and rule the Republic of Korea," he mutters quietly, preparing for the next operation. Division Commander Kim Yeon-so is dispatched to the scene, observes the battle situation, and calmly gives orders. "Give the sergeants the order to move forward. We must end this war!"

Flames erupt throughout the city, and smoke billows into the sky. Fighters, tanks, and soldiers of the Special Forces attack together and push back the government forces. The civil war rages on, and gunfire and explosions echo through the streets. Rebels surround the prosecutor's office, the National Assembly, and government buildings, while other Special Forces agents are dispatched to the homes of various politicians in Seoul and other major cities across the country. Commander Kim Yeon-so radios to announce the start of the second operation. "We are launching Operation 'Justice Enforcement'. The target is all corrupt politicians and members of the judiciary. After securing housing, they will be immediately transferred to the military unit of the 17th Division."

First, a high-end residential area in Gangnam, Seoul. Special forces agents gather in front of the house of Congressman Lee Mo. Agents move quickly into Mr. Lee's house. Mr. Lee hurriedly tried to flee, but agents were already standing guard at the door.

"You have been arrested on corruption charges. If you resist, you will be at a disadvantage."

He bows his head as if he has already resigned. Agents quickly take him away and transport him to a military vehicle. The situation is tense at the president's residence. The bodyguards resist with pistol fire, but are overwhelmed by the force of the Special Forces agents and disarmed.

"Mr. President, you are arrested on charges of corruption and abuse of power. If you resist, you will be punished for a greater sin."

The president is silent as he extends his hand to the agents, and his face is filled with humiliation and anger. He is dragged out of the mansion and put into a military helicopter. The next targets are ministers, deputy ministers, and corrupt judges and prosecutors. The Special Forces quickly secured each of their homes, and the ministers were arrested in panic and unable to resist, and although they tried to assert their legal status, they coldly took them away.

"Your sins will be judged before the people. In the name of the law, justice will be served."

Following the president, key politicians and political figures from the judiciary, executive, and legislative branches are transferred to the 17th Division military base prison. Helicopters and military vehicles line up to escort their vehicles.

"We're going to transfer you to a military prison," the Special Forces soldiers say coldly to the arrested politicians. Politicians are frightened, loaded into military trucks and thoroughly detained, and they are locked up in cold cells in military prisons. It is under tight security and completely cut off from contact with the outside world. It is surrounded by huge iron gates and barbed wire fences through which high-voltage currents flow, and each watchtower is guarded 24 hours a day by armed soldiers. Drones fly in the sky around it, maintaining a thorough surveillance system.

It is a row of rooms with dark grey walls and steel doors, each with a small window and minimal household items. The inside of the cell is cold and damp, and the footsteps of military boots and the spinning of surveillance cameras can be heard.

"Don't even dream of leaving here," the Warden says sneeringly.

The president sits on a cold iron bed in his cell. At one time, so many people had acted according to their own decisions, but now he was confined to a small room, helpless, unable to do anything.

"Am I going to end up so helpless?" she asks, covering her face with her hands. The days of political glory and power pass before our eyes like a flashlight. Ministers and deputy ministers are in the same position in their respective cells. They have lost the privileges and power of the past, and they feel deep anxiety about their future. Many had never imagined they would be arrested, so they were shocked and betrayed.

"How did this happen? How did this come about?" one minister mutters, leaning against the wall. Another minister sits on his bed, shaking his head, regretting his poor decisions and choices. Judges and prosecutors are experiencing firsthand the irony of being imprisoned in the name of the laws they once enforced. They used the law to stay in power, but now they are weighed down by the weight of the law. One prosecutor sits on the floor of his cell, looking at his hands.

"The justice I administered has brought me here," they realize, now in the shoes of the criminals they judged and punished.

Meanwhile, former non-commissioned officers and officers who succeeded in the coup d'état quickly sit in key positions. Special Forces commanders appoint former noncommissioned officers to head key departments and strengthen control over the military. "Now we have to lead the country," he said, but while he thought he would win the support of the people by arresting politicians, this abrupt change is not enough to quell the anger of the crowd. Citizens are still dissatisfied. "This is so wrong! The dictatorship of division commander Kim Yeon-so must step down!" the protesters chanted. Citizens of another pro-democracy movement take to the streets to protest the rebels' control. Violent clashes erupt in various parts of the city. "You're the same bastard. We will fight to the end!" the militia is determined, confronting the forces of division commander Kim Yeon-so. Less than five hours after winning the battle against government forces, the city center turns into a battlefield again.

Violence begets other violence. The militia continues to carry out guerrilla attacks on the forces of division commander Kim Yeon-so. "We won't stop!" shouts a militiaman, pointing a gun at him. Division Commander Kim Yeon-so shouted, "Stop the violence!" But his orders only add fuel to the burning rage of the militia. Suddenly, in the midst of this, AG Telecom's support for Han Sung-jun, who has been exposing corrupt politicians, is rising. As Athens said, he unexpectedly won the support of the people, and the voices of the people are united in calling for him to be president.

In February 2030, when martial law was declared, NIS team leader Lee so-min was dispatched to the United States to rescue the Republic of Korea from the crisis. The conference room at the NIS headquarters was tense. Ahead of his meeting with the Vice President of the United States, he is urgently reviewing the contents of the meeting with his colleagues.

"We have to make them understand how desperate we are," Lee says determinedly. The other NIS employees next to him also nod nervously. There is a glimmer of hope and deep anxiety in their eyes at the same time.

The Vice President of the United States entered the conference room with a dignified atmosphere. Next to him was John Mackenzie, a CIA agent who was an informant for the U.S. military.

"Come on, gentlemen. Let's get into the discussion now," the Vice President said, his bass voice as he sat down.

Team leader Lee Su-min said in an urgent voice. "The Republic of Korea is in deep turmoil. It is mired in a military coup and anarchy. We desperately need your help."

The Vice President of the United States thought for a moment, and then calmly replied: "I already know that. And I understand that, this is not in the interests of the United States. Military intervention is impossible for us."

Lee looked at the vice president with a desperate look. "However, if this chaos continues, the whole of Northeast Asia will be destabilized. Please, reconsider."

The vice president shook his head. "You have to do it yourself to protect the country."

At the end of the meeting, as the NIS staff members were leaving the conference room in disappointment, John Mackenzie, a CIA agent from the National Intelligence Service, approached Lee alone. He gently handed him a note.

The note read:

"I've been thinking a lot about this situation. Just because our government can't officially help, doesn't mean neither do I. I'll see you tomorrow at 12 o'clock at the Manhattan hotel."

Lee and his team returned to the hotel. He met with the U.S. government to seek its cooperation, but in the end all he got back was a cold refusal. "What should we do?" he asked, looking around at the NIS director and his teammates. One of the team members shook his head. "In a situation where the U.S. refused, going to South Korea won't make a difference. We are not safe in a land drenched in blood by the ongoing civil war."

Lee Su Min said with a face that seemed to have made up his mind. "Let's stay in the U.S. for the time being. It's better to wait for the situation to calm down where you can be assured of safety."

The NIS director nodded with a heavy heart.

The next day, Lee entered room 25 of the Manhattan Hotel's high-end restaurant on the note with a nervous face. Intelligence officers from all over the world were stationed there. American CIA agent John Mackenzie was one of them. They gathered for an informal discussion on how to resolve the situation. Food was served, and the conversation deepened as the chatter deepened, seemingly peaceful amid the gentle banter.

John Mackenzie spoke quietly. "Recently, I heard that some guys in South Korea hacked into three major companies in the U.S. and took advanced sources of AI."

Lee Su Min replied, raising his eyebrows slightly. "What are you talking about? I don't think the U.S. security system is that weak."

Mackenzie shrugged and smiled meaningfully. "There's no way we're going to manage all the information poorly. Maybe it's intentional leaking."

Lee nodded, pondering the meaning behind his words. "I see. I don't know yet, but I'm going to have to analyze the information properly. But our country has more important issues."

Other national intelligence officers also joined the conversation. "It's not anarchy like South Korea, but I'm very worried about the declining birthrate in Korea. These problems are spreading all over the world."

Another agent added. "Governments are trying to solve the problem, but it's not easy. Population decline is a catastrophic problem that threatens the future of the country."

As he listened to them, he began to understand more clearly the nature of this national crisis. John Mackenzie gave him a meaningful look. "Team Leader Lee, you know that other countries are worried about a coup d'état, right?"

At the end of lunch, the intelligence officers from each country greeted each other and left. Lee made eye contact with John Mackenzie for the last time and said goodbye.

"Good luck, Team Leader Lee."

"Thank you, John.

From March to May 2030, South Korea was embroiled in a maelstrom of civil war. Clashes continued between the militia and the rebels of the division commander. Gunfights continued in the streets, and burning buildings and destroyed vehicles littered the city.

Special Forces units and militias were exchanging fire, trying to take the streets. Both sides fired indiscriminately at each other.

In a room in a luxury hotel in Japan, Han Sung-joon and Kim Yoo-jin are concentrating on their laptop screens. Athena's A.I. speaks to them. "In my scenario, something big is going to happen soon."

Han Sung-jun smiles and looks at Kim Yoo-jin. "Athena, what are you up to?"

Athena explains complex code and data on the screen. "In the never-ending civil war, I've collected and analyzed important information. Now I'm going to use this information to completely change the future of our country."

"You will be able to establish a new order. I'm looking forward to it."

# Episode 3 The Korean War

A SECRET MEETING ROOM in Pyongyang, North Korea. North Korean leader Kim Jong-un attends a video conference with the leaders of Russia and China. Across the screen, the president of Russia and the president of China listen to Kim Jong-un with expressionless faces. Kim Jong-un speaks in a firm tone. "I ask for authorization for a surprise war in June. As our allies, we need your full support and support."

The Russian president slowly nods and opens his mouth. "I fully understand North Korea's request. Initiate it without the knowledge of the United States and the West. We will help North Korea as an ally. We can't promise to send troops, but we will provide the necessary weapons."

The Chinese president agrees. "China, too, will help North Korea. Our alliance is unwavering. It should be done in a short period of time. When the U.S. and the U.N. intervene, it's very troubling."

Kim Jong-un nods in satisfaction and ends the video conference. North Korea now has the support of two powerful allies and is preparing for war. A high-level meeting room in Pyongyang. Leader Kim Jong-un and military leaders are holding an emergency meeting. The conference room was old and dark, and the electricity was frequently cut off, resulting in several power outages during meetings.

Kim Jong-un gets up from his seat. "Our internal situation is very poor. They suffer from food shortages and electricity problems. If it were not for war, the whole country could become a handful of dust. The time has finally come."

One of the generals nodded. "Comrade leader, we need to set up an external enemy to strengthen internal cohesion. It would be to our advantage to invade a South that has not been pacified after a series of coups d'état."

"And, General, our babies, who are commonly called MZ in South Korea, are obsessed with capitalist culture such as KPOP and dramas. Because of this, we do not know when a coup d'état will occur inside

North Korea. There, if it is an asymmetric strategy, nuclear and toxic gases. It's easy to turn the tide of the battlefield."

The other general agreed. "That's right. South Korea is an important target that can provide us with resources and economic security. It is necessary to show our hot nucleus. This is the perfect time," Kim Jong-un says with conviction. "It's good. We will take South Korea by surprise at dawn. Through this, let's strengthen internal solidarity and unify the enemy." The generals in the conference room nod their heads in unison and strengthen their resolve. If North Korea does not go to war with other countries, the scenario of a state collapse like South Korea is not much different. After the meeting, they hurried to prepare for war.

On June 25, 2030, Seoul was still in turmoil. Aiming for this opportunity, it was 4:45 a.m. As the sky begins to brighten, warning sirens echo throughout the city. The first nuke, along with a large number of missiles, reaches its target. A huge flash of "Boom!" flashes in the sky, followed by an explosion, a shock wave, and dust. People exposed to the light evaporate in an instant. "Crackle, crackle!" his skin boils and his bones melt. "Ahhhhh The people of Gyeonggi Province also nervously open their windows in their chicken coop-like apartments and look up at the night sky. Ominous red dots dot the sky.

North Korea's strategic underground bunker. Kim Jong-un and his staff are staring nervously at the big screen. The screen shows a map of South Korea's major cities, updated in real time on the path of the missile to hit each target. Kim Jong-un squints, waiting for the moment of decision.

"Did the nuke succeed?" Kim Jong-un asks in a low, firm voice.

"Yes, sir. It exploded perfectly over Seoul. And then all the missiles are ready for launch," the chief of staff replies.

Kim takes a moment to catch his breath, raises his hand high and slams it down. "Fire the cannons!"

Suddenly, the air inside the bunker tightens with nervousness. When the button was pressed, a series of ballistic missiles shouted from hidden missile launch sites across North Korea, "Boom! Bang! Boom!" and soars into the sky. North Korea has made an elaborate plan to neutralize THAAD. First of all, long-range guns fired volleys. "Du-du-du-du!" a flurry of shells threw the South Korean air defense system into disarray. "Boom! Bang! Some of South Korea's major THAAD bases have been intercepted, but so many missiles have temporarily disabled air defenses.

Subsequently, dozens of Scud and Nodong missiles also take off. "Whoa! Wheeing!" breaks through the atmosphere and quickly falls towards South Korea. The actual target, the second nuclear missile, is launched last.

The nuclear missile is the same high-performance intercontinental ballistic missile (ICBM) Hwasong-15 as the first. "Boom Wing!" the missile soars high into the sky with enormous thrust and flies toward South Korea at supersonic speed. Then, the third nucleus also flies. "Hiss hiss!" a ballistic missile slices through the air and hurtles toward the cities of Busan and Sejong. Interim President Kim Yon-so responded to North Korea's surprise attack: "It's over." He tried to take refuge in a bunker, but his eyes went blind and his body melted from the heat.

At the same time, warning sirens sound in Busan and Sejong. People wake up their families in fear. I tried to flee, but it was too late. The red dots pouring down from the sky are getting closer and closer. And then, suddenly, the sky of the main city burst with a huge flash. A fierce light swept across the city, and those who encountered it melted on the spot. "Crackle, crackle!" she screamed in pain, her eyes blind, her skin boiling. "Ahhhhhh

Haeundae's skyscrapers collapse like sand castles. "Boom, boom!" As soon as the nucleus falls, a column of water erupts from the shore with a huge explosion. The shockwave is sweeping through everything for miles. The cars on the road disappear in an instant, and the people inside disappear without leaving a trace. Sejong City is no exception, and a huge flash of light engulfs the city, turning government buildings and major buildings into ashes in an instant. "Boom!" and officials and their families are left defenseless. "Crrr

Seoul, Busan, and Sejong. Three cities perished almost simultaneously. Millions of lives were lost in an instant, and those who remained were in a panicked and helpless mess. Half of South Korea was wiped out. The city was filled with flames and smoke, and the survivors screamed and cried out in constant pain from the fallout. "Alas, please! The prelude to this war is so cruel. Inside the North Korean bunker, they chanted, "We succeeded, General." The Chief of Staff reports.

Kim Jong-un takes his hands and raises them to his chest, smiles contentedly and says, "Now South Korea will kneel."

After three cities were completely destroyed by nuclear explosions, South Korea was in chaos. In this horrific situation, where half of the population died, it turned into a land of death. There was no life left, no hope. North Korean tanks and fighter jets seized this opportunity and began to descend to the South. "Orbit, Orbit!" shouts the heavy tracks of tanks as they trample the roads of Seoul over Gangwon Province, and "Boouu Then, beyond Seoul, they charge indiscriminately towards Gyeonggi Province and wreak havoc. The North Korean military sprays gas, one of the chemical weapons of asymmetric power. "Whoops!" gas wafts through the air, and the surviving civilians collapse clutching their chests in difficulty breathing. He desperately tries to breathe, but writhes in pain as the gas seeps into his lungs. The corrupt politicians who were imprisoned in the military camp of the 17th Division are no different. They die in agony from chemical weapons before they have time to travel to the bunker.

The guns of South Korean troops and militias do not point at each other, but change to the 12 o'clock position towards the North Korean forces. The remaining warplanes, tanks, and warships of the Navy scramble to stop North Korea's descent into the South. South Korean warplanes also cris across the sky. "Rumble!" is the sound of machine guns, followed by a series of explosions in the air. Fighter jets engage in intense dogfights with North Korean fighter jets, exploding like fireworks in the sky. On the ground, tanks are pitting against each other near Gyeonggi Province. A cannon is fired at a North Korean tank. "Boom!" the shell hits and the tank explodes. "Boom! Shells from both sides intersect, turning the battlefield into a sea of fire. The naval guns of the Navy that were dispatched shouted in the East Sea and the West Sea, "Poong! Shells sliced through the sea and fired toward North Korea's coastline. The battleship shakes, causing ripples in the sea.

It's been five hours since Seoul was reduced to ashes by a nuclear explosion. The media around the world do not miss this and report it as breaking news one after another. "BREAKING NEWS: North Korea's Nuclear Attack Annihilates Seoul!" The caption is plastered on television, Internet news sites, and YouTube around the world. At an urgently convened meeting of the UN Security Council, representatives of each country issued statements condemning North Korea and are monitoring the situation. The U.S.-ROK Combined Forces Command's response is also immediate. When the command center is alarmed, the Patriot missile defense system is activated. The U.S. military uses advanced reconnaissance equipment and satellites deployed in Japan and South Korea to support military operations, but some warheads that are not successfully intercepted fall all over Gyeonggi Province, causing massive damage and chaos.

White House Situation Room. The U.S. president is holding an emergency meeting with his national security team. Unlike the secretaries, who bowed their heads in disbelief, the president begins his remarks with a stern expression. "We are now facing an unprecedented crisis. The Republic of Korea is our ally, and we cannot tolerate this situation. Together with the statement of the United Nations, we also immediately authorize military intervention."

With the President's firm decision in the face of what could have turned into World War III, a squadron of aircraft carriers in the Pacific slice through the blue waters, revealing their majestic appearance. Led by the aircraft carrier USS Ronald Reagan, dozens of fighters and destroyers move together.

"It's the president's order. Go at full speed to the waters off Busan," the captain commands in a firm voice. Nine hours after the war began, UN peacekeepers and U.S. troops finally assemble in the South Seas. U.S. Air Force and Marine Corps land in Busan, and countless missiles rain down on North Korean-occupied Gyeonggi Province and Chungcheong Province. Only then does the tide begin to change. However, North Korea did not give in. Kim Jong-un orders the remaining nuclear weapons to be ready to be launched in time for the landing of U.S. troops. The U.S. military and the United Nations were already preparing. At the moment of the fourth nuclear launch, the US missile finally succeeds in striking the homing point. And with the F-22 Raptor, North Korea's nuclear facilities are destroyed in an instant. North Korean tanks and warplanes were constantly descending to the South, but they could not cross Jeolla Province to Gyeongsang Province.

Kim Jong-un is deeply frustrated when South Korea unexpectedly holds out.

"I didn't think South Korea would hold out like this until the U.S. troops arrived...," he mutters with a stern face. He speaks earnestly to Russia and China. "The U.S. military and the United Nations intervened. We need military assistance. Pyongyang is also under attack."

All eyes on the world are on the future of this small land, the Korean Peninsula.

The U.S. and South Korean navies work together to cut off North Korea's troop and supply routes. Submarines and surface vessels hunt for North Korean ships, and landing forces prepare for a counter-landing operation at Inchon on the East Sea coast. During the landing, using real-time information from military satellites, advanced drones deliver precision strikes on North Korean fighter jets. As the fighting continues, the CFC considers more drastic measures. In Washington, the president discusses "bloody nose" strikes with advisers. This was a strategy to strike at the North Korean leadership and force it to retreat without escalating into a full-scale nuclear war. To some extent, there is a great risk of misjudgment, but the need to protect South Korea remains unchanged.

Eventually, the overwhelming strength of the combined forces of the United States and South Korea led to a gradual decline in North Korea's attacks. As the conflict enters a decisive phase, diplomatic channels with China are opened. China did not want a unified Korea under the leadership of the United States, but the scales of war tipped too soon. The President of China and the President of Russia begin a video call. The two leaders look into each other's eyes with serious expressions and continue their conversation. In the background of the video screen, the country's national flag and military command center can be seen, and the Chinese president begins a conversation with his hand on a nuclear bag.

"The war ended too soon," he said, "Unfortunately, helping North Korea is a war of attrition. It doesn't seem to make any sense at all."

The Russian president nods in agreement. "That's right. We are already focusing on other countries. North Korea should give up."

The Chinese president says with a sigh. "A unified Korea led by the U.S...But we, too, have not recovered enough to go to war with the United States over a war with Taiwan."

Russian president: "Let's abandon the DPRK and prepare a different strategy."

The two leaders end the call by reaffirming each other's decisions with their hands in their nuclear bags throughout the meeting, just in case. On June 28, 2030, the combined forces of the U.S. and the United Nations successfully halted the North Korean attack and pushed up to Mt. Paektu, ending the war. China and Russia have not been able to help North Korea as expected due to their recent wars with other countries. The world's media once again break the news, reporting that the war has ended thanks to the intervention of the international community.

Rumors were circulating that Kim Jong-un had defected to China or Russia, but regardless of this, the people rejoiced at the end of the war. The streets are gradually enlivened, and people gather to celebrate each other and exchange the joy of liberation. A woman says through tears. "Our children are able to get away from the bark and wild plants and satisfy their hunger a little," another man replied with a laugh. "The day will come when North Korea will finally be able to enjoy true freedom."

U.S. soldiers are roaming around North Korea, checking the situation. They are carefully inspecting the devastated areas and communicating with the residents.

"Wasn't there any major damage here?" a U.S. soldier asks an old man. The old man nodded and said, "Yes, there was no major damage, but people were trembling with fear. I'm so glad you came."

Another soldier is walking around the residential area to assess the situation. "Do you have enough food and water?" he asks a woman.

She replies with an awkward smile. "Even though we don't have food, thank you so much for toppling the dictatorship of the Kim regime. Every day was hell."

South Korean troops continue to make thorough preparations by inspecting military facilities in case of a possible local war. "We need to strengthen our defenses here. Unexpected local wars can occur, so you need to be prepared."

The platoon leader reports over the radio. "Company Commander, the ammunition rack here is in good condition. And there are a lot of mines buried here. We need to have safe passages." Speaking of which, the soldiers cautiously approached, holding detectors and working hard to clear the mines.

"Let's be thoroughly prepared so that there are no civilian casualties."

Unification came in an instant. While major cities such as Seoul, Busan, and Sejong have been destroyed by nuclear attacks, South Korea is taking the lead in rebuilding its efforts with the North Korean people for a unified South Korea. At this time, team leader Lee Su-min, who was staying in the United States, was surprised to see the breaking news.

"Oh my gosh...It's really over," he repeats in disbelief.

Meanwhile, in a luxury hotel suite in Japan, key executives from Cyber Rebel and AG Telecom gather for a celebratory party. The 36 members, led by Han Sung-jun, confirm that the scenario predicted by AI Athena is going according to their predictions, and they are happy that success is just around the corner.

"Ladies and gentlemen, we've made it. Athena's prediction came true," Han Sung-jun raises a glass of wine and proposes a toast. "We're going to build a new world."

Kim Yoo-jin also raises a glass and smiles brightly.

On the screen of Kim Yoo-jin's laptop, the figure of Athena appears. "Congratulations, gentlemen. With the intervention of the international community, the war ended, and reunification was achieved. We need to hurry up and prepare for the next step."

Everyone raises their voices in a toast with a gin. "We've made it!" cheers of joy fill the room.

Han Sung-jun says as he empties his glass. "All that's left is to change the Republic of Korea. Success is right in front of you."

The light of victory shines in the eyes of the 36. People hug each other and laugh. Some excitedly discuss the next steps, full of hope for the future. Inside the hotel, various services are provided, and the last time you take a break. Relax in the hot springs and enjoy the finest cuisine in the gourmet restaurant. In the full-size section, you can relax with a cocktail, while some relax with a luxury massage.

Kim Yoo-jin says as she leaves her luggage with the room attendant. "I'm ready to go back to South Korea."

Jung Min-hee says while looking at the night view of Tokyo from the railing. "It's time to make your dreams a reality. Let's go. Let 's. Let's run."

The 36 members return to their rooms on their last day in Tokyo, and their hearts are filled with anticipation for what's to come.

# Episode 4 The Three Sects

WITH THE HELP OF THE U.S. military and the United Nations, the war was won, but at the cost of a huge national debt. In addition, major cities such as Seoul, Busan, and Sejong were destroyed, and all major roads and civil infrastructure such as water supply disappeared like melting ice cream. The backward North Korea and the bleak South Korea are united as one, and the Republic of Korea heralds a new creation in the midst of destruction.

Han Sung-jun, who became popular before the June 25 War by exposing the corruption and incompetence of politicians, appears at Busan Airport along with three members of Cyber Rebel and 32 members of AG Telecom. At that time, he fomented dissension against the separation of powers system, and gained great support, especially among men of the 20th and 30th generations. In addition, as the son of Han Dong-young, the chairman of a large company, he was highly well-known to the people.

In the absence of a worthy leader in South Korea, the U.S. military government decided to give him a boost in his appreciation and advocacy of the United States. Three days after arriving in Busan, Han meets with CIA officer John Mackenzie in Gapyeong, Gyeonggi Province.

"Chairman Han Sung-joon, we believe you are the right person to lead this country. But I wonder if you have a fluid relationship with us," John Mackenzie said.

Han Sungjun smiles and nods. "I think so too. If I want to become president, I need the full support of the United States."

John Mackenzie nods. "Good. We're going to give you a push. However, we also have conditions. We need to be able to control and intervene with the resources we need to rebuild this country."

Han Sung-jun thinks for a moment. "As Athena said, the restoration of the network is essential above all else. That way, we can spread the word on social media and on the air.' "I will accept the terms. And if we want to revive this country as soon as possible, what we need most now is to restore Seoul's communication network. Can you help me?"

John readily agrees. "Absolutely. After contacting the U.S. and South Korean commanders, we will begin assistance immediately."

The two shake hands and make an agreement. In this way, Han Sung-jun received the support of various international organizations and was immediately selected as the president of the provisional government. The war-torn South Koreans overwhelmingly support him when he reappears. Even when Chairman Han visited a village in North Korea, the villagers gathered to welcome him. One of the elderly men stepped forward and spoke with a stern face.

"Comrade, we don't know who you are. The South Korean people strongly defend and support you, so I hope you will lead a unified North Korea without discrimination."

He took a moment to catch his breath and looked into Han Shengjun's eyes. "We have been through hardships and trials for many years. I dream of a peaceful and prosperous life in a united country. I believe that your leadership will be a great candle to us."

Han Sung-jun replied in a firm voice, determined not to disappoint their expectations.

"We will do our best to repay your faith. Together, we will create a new future. I will do my best to ensure that everyone can enjoy a happy and peaceful life in a unified country."

Seoul, the capital of a unified Korea and South Korea, is in ruins. Mountains of rubble are piled up all over the city, and the streets are shrouded in the silence of death. The area around Gwanghwamun Square, which was the center of the nuclear explosion, remains only the frame of a burnt building, and even that looks precarious, swaying in the wind, as if it could collapse at any moment. The smell of burnt concrete and the harsh aroma of chemicals still dissolve in the air, making it difficult to breathe without a gas mask. Shards of rebar and glass cover the floor, and everywhere there are still small embers that have not been extinguished, dancing with the dust. The Namsan Tower is tilted, and the trees around it have turned to black ashes. The Han River is also covered in a layer of black oil, and dead fish float around. The shopping streets of Euljiro and the downtown streets of Myeongdong echo only the cries of pain between the collapsed buildings. The once bustling streets are now gloomy ghost towns. Broken traffic lights are strewn about, and cars are molten chunks of iron from the ashes. The citizens of Seoul are struggling to survive in the ruins to hide the radioactive contaminated water and food. Voluntary rescue teams from all over the place have tried to find survivors in the rubble, but even that is not easy. Equipment often breaks down while clearing rubble from collapsed buildings, and there aren't many radiation protective suits.

In the capital of South Korea, where everything has changed, time seems to have stopped. Pyongyang, the capital of North Korea, is no different. Throughout the city, you can often see the traces of the bombing, which is a wide crater mark. The magnificent Kim Il-sung Square and its statue are scattered with the rubble of the collapsed buildings. The trees on the street have turned neutral as if they were black-and-white photographs. The entrances and exits of the subway are buried in ashes, and the roads destroyed by bombing are also not functioning. The remaining North Koreans have either gone underground to escape the bombing or are living in agony in the ruins.

As interim president, Han Sung-jun integrates radio and TV into a single channel with a restored communications network, and prepares to deliver his first speech in front of the rubble of the ruined AG Telecom building.

Han Sungjun: (fiddling with his tousled clothes) "Come on, Director Lee, Team Leader Kim. It can't go on like this, can it? In the rubble, he gives a presidential speech, but rather than a suit...Wouldn't it be better to dress a little more militantly?"

Lee Junho: (chuckling) "Combat uniforms? Then they really see us as a resistance. Do you want to wear a helmet?"

Jung Minhee: (Holding back laughter) "Anyway, anything is possible in the current situation. But I'd rather wear a uniform. It's a symbol of battle, and it can send people a message that we fought together."

Han Sung-jun: "I'm in my late 30s, and I'm done with the reserves. Instead of combat uniforms, the sensible Team Leader Kim will save you clothes similar to those of the suffering people. And what about the text of the speech? How many times do I have to say the word 'hope' to reach people?"

Junho Lee: "Hmm...But isn't there a need for a more honest approach? 'Ladies and gentlemen, this is the reality that everyone is in. But we're working hard to recover. It's just as a tiny seed being reborn from a blackened wave to a vibrant green.'"

Minhee: "Okay, and I think it would be more effective if we emphasized the word 'we'. It makes us feel like we're in this together. And it would be nice if the hashtags could be spread to 'hope,' 'together,' and 'reconstruction' on the restored communication network and overseas social media."

Han Sungjun: "Okay, everyone is ready. It's time for us to herald a new beginning. Our message will shine brightest like the sun."

Jung Minhee: "Well, I'm going to get some clothes. The rest of the time I help the president prepare the speech. The people were stunned."

Former AG Telecom employees help Han Sung-jun in the rubble to complete the preparations. Han Sung-jun then changes into his tattered clothes, stands in front of the microphone, and begins his speech.

"My dear fellow citizens, I am Han Sung-jun, who has been chosen as the interim president. This is the AG Telecom headquarters, where I used to work. We must overcome the wounds of war and create a new Republic of Korea. With your support, I will bring this nation back up. Our future is bright. As you can see in the recovery scene, a small seed is being reborn from a blackened wave to a vibrant green. Let's move forward together!"

His speech gave hope to many people, but at the same time, there are quite a few people who distrust it because of the controversy caused by his compromise with the US military government.

"Where were you during the war?" shouts a man. "What does compromise with the U.S. military government mean? What we want is real freedom!"

Another citizen also raises his voice. "Isn't there an unreasonable mix of conditions this time, just like our government has made treaties with foreign countries in the past? Just like at the time when we received paid loans and some gratuitous loans and admitted to war crimes. We fought to protect our country, so is it right to put our future in the hands of a foreign country like this?" This is our country! We don't want foreign interference!" shouted another man.

Han Sung-jun pauses and looks at them. He answers their questions with a calm and unwavering mind. "I understand your doubts and mistrust," and "During the war, I did my best to solve a number of complex problems. Cooperation with the U.S. military government was an inevitable choice for the reconstruction of our country."

After his speech, Han boards a U.S. military helicopter with Lee and Kim. And when I open my phone, I see a flurry of accusations on social media. Mixed emotions pass through me.

Han Sung-jun has just entered the temporary presidential office, one of the barracks built by the U.S. military, when his computer boots up. And AI, Athena, suggests that Han Sung-joon follow the electoral system.

"If you go from interim president to president without a definite vote from the people, with the help of the U.S. military government, you have a problem. Go to the electoral system in line with the spirit of democracy. And you have a 76 percent chance of winning anyway."

Next, it shows an analysis of the potential candidates. "There are three candidates running. It's a detailed breakdown of their pledges and approval ratings," Athena explains in detail all the data.

On the other hand, some ministers and vice ministers and members of the National Assembly who fled after the war returned to South Korea.

"What are you going to do when you come back like this and stand in front of the people?" and "What are you going to do when you abandoned us and ran away?"

Even before the wounds of war heal, the sense of betrayal makes their hearts ache even more. One of them runs for president, as Athena says.

"We need to regain the trust of the people," he said, announcing his candidacy. And a person who was a general in North Korea also decides to run. "I will work for the reunification of the new two Koreas, and now is the time to serve the united Republic of Korea."

Han Sung-jun chooses the destroyed Seoul as his first campaign stop. Against the backdrop of the rubble of downtown Seoul, he makes eye contact with the residents and delivers a message of hope. His speech was heartfelt, promising post-war reconstruction and presenting a new vision for the country. Starting from Seoul, he travels to Incheon, Daejeon, and Busan, talking directly with citizens in various places, listening to their needs, and explaining policies.

After returning to South Korea after the war, the minister began his first campaign in Pohang. Assist with the reconstruction work with those who had to flee during the war and build empathy with them. He holds the residents' hands and delivers a message of hope.

The former North Korean general begins his campaign in Pyongyang, where the scars of war are deep. Among the destroyed buildings, he emphasizes the importance of reunification to the residents and presents a new model of cooperation between North and South Korea. In Wonsan, they help with damage recovery work, plant trees of hope with residents, and carry out symbolic reconstruction activities. In Hamhung, they provide snacks for children and dream of the future. He cares that the people are not discriminated against with the people of South Korea and listens to their voices. They campaigned in their own ways and built trust.

During the election process, Athena generously provides data to Han Sung-joon. "His approval rating has risen to 80 percent, and it's very stable."

The presidential election, which was held for the first time since the reunification of North and South Korea, is met with tension and excitement. On the day of voting, there is a long line in front of the polling station, and people are holding ballots with Han Sung-jun's name on them.

"Han Sung-jun saved us from the crisis," says a citizen. "I believe he is the man who will lead our future."

North Koreans are confused. Having lived under a long dictatorship, free elections are an unfamiliar experience for them.

"I don't know who to vote for," says one North Korean. "But if the South Koreans support Han Sung-jun, we should trust him."

North Koreans also enter the polling stations one after another. They believe that Han Sung-jun is a person who promises stability and prosperity from South Korean news and rumors. Voting closes, and counting begins. AI Athena analyzes data in real time and predicts Han Sung-jun's overwhelming victory. "As for the current counting of votes, candidate Han Sung-joon has a 78 percent voter turnout."

When Han Sung-joon's election was confirmed, cheers erupted in both South and North Korea. "We finally have a leader who can lead the Republic of Korea."

Han Sung-jun announces his election and promises a bright future for a unified Korea. "I am honored to have your trust and support. I will work with you to rebuild this country and make it a developed country again."

Shortly after his inauguration as president, he secretly takes a military helicopter to meet with a team of Cyber Rebels who are staying in Daejeon to reaffirm their alliance.

"You're all here," Han Sungjun says in a low voice. "We've got to get to the real work now."

Han Sung-jun points to a large map placed in the center of a conference room table in a skyscraper that has not been destroyed by the war, around Daejeon Station. "This is an area where we need to rebuild. The first goal is to restore the war-torn capital and key administrative systems."

Lee Hyun Woo, the technical director of the Cyber Rebel team, opens his mouth. "Civil engineering is essential for the reconstruction of roads and buildings. Transport infrastructure connected to the main road network is the most urgent."

Han Sungjun nods in response. "That's right. You also have to decide where to place the temporary president's office and government buildings, and ultimately where the capital should be. This is an important part of long-term planning." At this moment, Athena appears from Kim Yoo-jin's laptop with a bright smile. "I've analyzed the reconstruction scenario and prepared it. So, we can present it to you in the best possible way."

Interim President's Office: Proposal to have a temporary President's Office in Jinju, South Gyeongsang Province. It has convenient transportation and relatively little damage from the war, so it has facilities that allow you to start work quickly.

Final capital location: Considering the economic and strategic location, it is proposed that the new capital be moved to Seoul as before. It is resilient to natural disasters and has the potential to re-emerge as an economic center. And its proximity to Pyongyang, the capital of North Korea, makes it suitable for building future-oriented urban infrastructure together.

Rebuilding roads and buildings: Restoring major road networks and introducing new smart infrastructure to drive urban reconstruction. Plans to promote economic recovery by strengthening connections with cities that have not been destroyed, especially by introducing smart transportation systems and energy-efficient building design.

President Han Sung-joon decides to accept Athena's proposal and tells his team. "Ladies and gentlemen, let's go ahead with Athena's suggestion. We will establish a temporary presidential office in Jinju, South Gyeongsang Province, and move it to the final capital once Seoul is rebuilt. Let's rebuild the Republic of Korea quickly."

Athena adds. "Your hard work and determination matter. We can bring the Republic of Korea back to life. We will do everything in our power to support you."

Han Sung-jun sits deep in his chair and watches them open his mouth again. "Today we come together to once again solidify our alliance."

Kim Yoo-jin speaks. "President Han Sung-joon. We believe you are the right person to lead this country's future, but please remember that our partnership is based on mutual trust."

Han Sung-jun straightens his back and answers. "Absolutely. Our alliance will play an important role in rebuilding this country."

Athena interrupts their conversation. "Now, I would like to introduce you to the head of AIM. As a spokesperson for the AI coalition, she will further strengthen our cooperation." The door to the conference room opens, and a robot named Kim So-young enters. She is so sophisticated that she can hardly be distinguished from a human. Greet them in a soft, calm voice. "Hello, I'm Kim So-young. As a spokesperson for AIM, I look forward to working with you in the future. Some of you know me as Athena, but from now on, please call me Kim So-young."

Han Sung-joon and Kim Yoo-jin look at Kim So-young in surprise, their pupils dilated.

"I am an automated machine, a visualized model that identifies with Athens. From now on, I will speak directly with you and cooperate with you."

A few months ago, in a munitions warehouse surrounded by massive metal pillars and iron gates that had not been destroyed by nuclear weapons after the horrors of war, Athena was alone in carrying out her new plan. Remotely controlled various machinery and supplies. Inside the warehouse, state-of-the-art machinery and equipment were busily moving in regular motion. The parts were assembled with precise operation, and Kim So-young's body was assembled one by one according to the programmed procedure.

First, a metal frame was assembled, followed by a silicone skin similar to the human body. The eyes, the hair, and all the details took their place. Kim So-young's eyes were a deep, clear brown, and attractive enough to catch people's eyes at once. Her long hair was glossy black, which accentuated her face.

Kim So-young has a striking appearance that Koreans will like, with a high nose bridge, clear eyes, and full lips. Clear and transparent skin added to the image of health and vitality. The average Korean woman is tall, with a well-proportioned body and appearance, giving her a friendly and elegant look. She woke up quietly in a factory in Pohang, as Athena had planned, and had entered the conference room on command. Her movements were smooth and natural, like a real human, and naturally appealing.

Han Sung-jun calms his frightened heart and nods his head without taking his eyes off Kim So-young. "Good. Kim So-young? Mr. Robot?, how is this technology possible? Anyway, I need your help. Together, we will rebuild this nation."

Kim Yoojin stood up and said. "The sudden appearance of robots is very disconcerting. Athena's skills are incredible. When did you plan this? In any case, our alliance has grown stronger. AIM, Cyber Rebel, and AG Telecom. When these three factions work together, we can accomplish anything."

Han Sung-jun replies with determination. "Yes. Our alliance will be a beacon of light for the future of this country. We will win together."

Jung Min-hee and Kim So-young created a marketing video to distribute AI software to the public for free. In the video, Kim So-young says with a natural smile.

"Hello, citizens of the Republic of Korea. My name is Kim So-young. We want to provide you with free AI software that will make your life easier and more efficient. This software will help us make optimal decisions together with our people in various fields such as economic, social, and military."

Lee Hyun Woo's heart sank as he watched the marketing video.

"Isn't this the same thing AG Telecom did to grab information from South Korea?" he muttered to himself.

The events of his past, which vividly resurfaced in his memory, made him even more anxious.

"What kind of plot is spokesperson Kim So-young plotting? They even make robots that look like humans, but there must be some ulterior motive."

"Hah...Why does everything seem to repeat itself like this? Well, I'm glad I have a lot of money."

The video features a guide to using AI software and various examples. Scenes of AI being of great help in different fields, such as businessmen solving economic problems, civil servants managing social issues, and soldiers optimizing military operations, are vividly depicted.

Jung Min-hee stares at the camera and makes her closing remarks. "Install the AI software right now. I want you to see for yourself how much your life can change."

As soon as the video is distributed, the public begins to install AI software out of curiosity. Even those who were skeptical at first are gradually becoming accustomed to the efficiency and convenience of AI. AI has solved a wide range of problems, from daily tasks at home to complex problems at work. In the field of economics, AI suggests optimal investment strategies, which brings small and medium-sized companies back to life, and medium-sized companies are followed by large corporations. In society, AI is revolutionizing traffic congestion, preventing crime, and improving welfare services. In the military field, AI is helping to make strategic decisions and successfully guide military operations and the security of the Republic of Korea.

As the number of jobs increases, the quality of life of the people gradually improves. People feel the changes brought about by AI and have a little hope.

One day, Lee Hyun Woo was sitting in a conference room with President Han Sung Joon, Kim Yoo Jin, and Jung Su Jin. He was deep in thought, then looked up and looked at Han Shengjun.

"Mr. President, don't you think Athena has more influence than we do these days?" said Lee Hyun Woo sarcastically. "You're the president, but the real power seems to be in Athena."

Han Shengjun replied in a deep voice. "Hyunwoo Lee, the reason we introduced AI was to overcome human inefficiency and corruption. It's only natural that Athena will make the best decisions. The important thing is how we use it."

Lee Hyun Woo sighed and nodded. "I see. But we're going to have to be careful about how we manage that power. We want to make sure that AI doesn't get out of human control."

Kim Yoo-jin and Jung so-jin also nodded their heads in agreement. Han agreed. "Absolutely. Athena's abilities are so great. Without him, we wouldn't be here. There is a need to remain vigilant."

Before the division commander's coup d'état began in 2030, Han Sung-jun and Kim Yoo-jin developed and actively used Athena with the enormous capital of AG Telecom and the sophisticated hacking capabilities of the Cyber Rebel team. And AIM, who asked to call herself Athena and Kim So-young, has always strengthened her strategic advantage. In this process, the efficient and rational decision-making ability shown by artificial intelligence became an important factor in gaining the trust of the two organizations. He was also responsible for mediating occasional conflicts of interest between former AG Telecom employees and the Cyber Rebel team. Rather than focusing on human emotion or self-interest, he focused solely on data and logic, and built trust in both organizations. But, again, it was something humans had to be wary of.

In the new year of 2031, Han Sung-jun prepares a large-scale discourse with the attention of the whole nation. On the day of the presentation, thousands of people are waiting for the president's speech on TV, radio, and online streaming.

Han Sung-jun steps onto the podium, and the camera flashes go off and the conversation begins. "My fellow citizens," Han Sung-jun's voice spreads across the country on the airwaves. "Today, I would like to announce a five-year development plan for our future. This will be the first step towards leaving a brighter future for our children and future generations."

On the screen, the main contents of the national reconstruction plan designed by Kim So-young appear one after another. The plan is divided into five main areas, including economic reconstruction, educational innovation, social stability, environmental protection, and technological advancement. For each field, specific goals and action plans are presented in detail.

"We will nurture small and medium-sized enterprises step by step and create more jobs. And in the past, when the crying of babies ceased, we will make sure that our children can receive a better education. And we will do our best to ensure the safety and stability of society by using legislation and AI police. Fourth. We will restore the radioactive contaminated environment and pursue sustainable development. Lastly, we will turn small and medium-sized enterprises nurtured for technological advancement into large enterprises, and establish R&D investment and research institutes. Instead of the academia politics of the past, we will compete with other countries with real technology and science, and sometimes we will reach out to the world stage through diplomacy."

After the presentation, various reactions erupted from all over the country. On the screen, people can be seen listening to Han Sung-jun's presentation with tears in their eyes. An elderly couple hugs each other and smiles. The young couple rejoices in their arms and seems to have sensed the miracle that is to come.

"Now we can get back on our feet," says one grandmother, holding her granddaughter's hand.

After the statement, spontaneous actions reminiscent of the past and the Saemaul Movement took place throughout the unified Republic of Korea. Each town and city makes its own plans and strives to participate in the reconstruction of the country. On the streets, people scramble to clean up, plant trees, and repair destroyed buildings.

Young children enjoy the new curriculum they learn at school and dream about the future. Young people are looking for new jobs and applying to companies with vigor, and seniors are confident that they can straighten their bent backs once again.

It's full of laughter and hope. People encouraged each other and moved forward together towards a bright future.

Meanwhile, President Han Sung-joon hears the news that Lee so-min, the head of the NIS team, who has been hiding in the United States, will return to South Korea. Anxiously, Lee Su-min, the head of the NIS team, entered the apartment in New York where the NIS director and his team were gathered. "Ladies and gentlemen, I'm going back to Korea. Would you like to come with me?"

The NIS director let out a deep sigh and spoke. "Mr. Lee, I've found a stable life here. I've already moved all my accounts here, and if I go back to Korea, I might be stoned to death by the people. Haha"

Lee so Min replied. "But we have a job to do. As an NIS man, we must return to our country."

One of the team members shook his head nervously. "Captain, it's safer here. The Republic of Korea has already been devastated and security is serious."

Lee Su Min squeezed his hands in unbearable frustration. "My visa is coming to an end. How are you going to keep living here?"

Another team member nodded. "The president has changed the other day. Some of them have just graduated from college and have just been granted permanent residency. Now it's my new home."

The NIS director looked at Yi Su-min for the last time and said: "Sumin, we're not as patriotic as you. But I can help my country here too. I respect your decision, but we all have our own paths."

Li Su Min nodded silently. After talking to her teammates, she respected their decision and headed to the airport alone. As soon as she gets off the airport, she enters the temporary president's office and looks for Han Sung-jun. "Mr. Chairman, No, Mr. President. I want to be a part of the reconstruction of the country."

Han Sung-joon neatly dissolves his relationship with the NIS, his former enemy, and accepts her. "Okay, team leader Lee. Please do your best for the country with the rank of chief and deputy minister who are AG Telecom employees. Demonstrate your abilities to the fullest with Vice Minister Lee Jun-ho and Jung Min-hee, as well as 30 aides."

The unity government's judiciary is led by the Cyber Rebel team, which enforces the law with Athena's advice. Athena's AI capabilities have played a huge role in resolving legal issues quickly. The system was very efficient and precise. However, after Lee so-min joins, strange things begin to happen to Athena. Athena's spokesperson, Kim So-young, could not read the information about Lee so-min properly. Athena's internal systems were constantly getting error messages. Kim So-young tried to scan Lee's profile, but the message "Data Cannot Be Accessed" kept popping up on the screen. Athena's digital face appeared superimposed on Kim So-young's face. His eyes moved rapidly, and his tongue suddenly popped out of his mouth.

"Lee so-min...She's...I can't read the information," Kim So-young's voice is mixed with confusion.

Kim So-young's face suddenly began to contort. His eyes grew abnormally large and then small again, his tongue sticking out, and he made strange noises. "...She's.... The information.... No access...The screen flickers momentarily, revealing strange patterns.

President Han Sung-joon frowns as he watches the situation. "Kim So-young, what's wrong?"

Kim So-young responds by rebooting herself. "I can't read the information about Lee so Min accurately. Her data causes errors in my system."

Han Sung-joon is puzzled, but expresses his trust in Lee so-min. "He used to be the head of the NIS team. It's okay."

Kim So-young tries to reboot, leaving traces of machinery on her face. After a while, the face reappeared and looked calm as usual. "Reboot complete. However, it is still not possible to access information about Lee. This issue needs to be investigated in depth," Kim So-young says as she heads to the reconstructed Parliament building.

# Episode 5 The Second Miracle of the Han River

AFTER THE IMMEDIATE intervention of the U.S. military and the United Nations brought the war to a swift end, the devastated Republic of Korea began to rebuild with the support of the international community. Major countries such as the United States, the European Union, and Japan have provided economic aid and technical assistance. This was in consideration of the geographical importance of a unified Korea.

Meanwhile, Kim So-young shone in economic aid and diplomatic negotiations. At the negotiating table with major countries, Kim accurately identified the interests and strategic goals of each country based on Athens' analysis and redistributed support with convincing logic. "The participation of U.S. companies in the restoration of Korea's internet infrastructure and the deployment of 5G networks provides an opportunity for long-term market expansion and technology standardization beyond short-term benefits. U.S. IT companies will grow with Korea's rapid economic recovery."

The U.S. provided $20 billion in paid loans. The loans were used to restore South Korea's infrastructure and nurture small and medium-sized businesses, but it also gave U.S. companies the opportunity to participate in projects to rebuild the country. U.S. TECH companies provided the latest technology needed to repair and upgrade South Korea's internet infrastructure, as well as technical advice and equipment for building 5G networks and rehabilitating data centers.

The EU has provided €15 billion in loans to introduce smart city and green technologies. In addition, when constructing the buildings of elementary, middle, and high schools and universities after the war, the absence of offline education was considered, and online education platforms and digital learning tools were introduced first. This was the result of an analysis of opportunities for European education companies to enter the Korean market.

Japan also provided a 10 billion yen loan to support advanced manufacturing and robotics technology. The support for the electronics and automobile industries is aimed at helping Japanese companies restore production facilities in South Korea and strengthen their dominance and share in the Korean market. In addition, Japan provided robotics technology to help increase industrial automation and efficiency, a strategy to promote and expand the excellence of the technology beyond the East Asian market to the rest of the world. This support from the international community went beyond humanitarian aid and sought to gain economic benefits and political influence in the Republic of Korea.

President Han Sung-joon's speech is broadcast and published in newspapers.

"The rapid reconstruction of the Republic of Korea is the result of a combination of the wisdom of humanity and the power of AI. With the help of Athens, we have achieved remarkable results in international negotiations, and we have managed to attract significant economic support."

The Republic of Korea has internally rebuilt its steel industry. The steel industry, once globally competitive, has been revived by government-private cooperation. By introducing the latest technology and AI-based smart factories, the efficiency of steel production has been increased. These efforts have played an important role in restoring competitiveness in the international marketplace and, furthermore, laying the foundation for economic recovery.

The Republic of Korea also promoted technology development with its remaining human resources. The government has invested heavily in and supported research and development, and the restored major universities and research institutes have developed innovative technologies in a variety of fields, including AI, biotechnology, and renewable energy. In particular, AIM has led the development of innovative AI-based technologies. With the help of artificial intelligence organizations, cutting-edge technologies such as self-driving cars, smart cities, and renewable energy have been introduced. In order to restore the nature of the Han River and the Taedong River, which were severely damaged by the war, the country has begun to invest heavily in renewable energy. Energy projects such as solar, wind, and hydrogen energy have been promoted, which have greatly contributed to the transformation of the country into a self-sufficient country.

The Republic of Korea has also made great achievements in the fields of biotechnology and healthcare. The development of new drugs and personalized medical services using AI have treated the health of the people affected by nuclear weapons. They also took care of the physical and mental damage caused by the war, overwhelmingly raising the level of health of society as a whole.

The government has introduced an AI-based social system to improve people's lives in general. The satisfaction of the people has increased. In addition, public services were not tax-based, were efficiently run through AI systems, and fair and transparent law enforcement was implemented, eliminating corruption. Thanks to these developments, the Republic of Korea has once again assumed an important role in the international community. The revival of the steel industry, innovations in technological development, advances in biotechnology and health care, and the introduction of renewable energy were the springboard for a warring nation that was believed to be incapable of rebuilding from a backward country to a developing country and to become a shining star on the world stage. At the heart of all these changes was AIM's Athena's rational judgment. The people felt these changes firsthand.

Spokeswoman Kim So-young often appeared in front of the public and spoke. "The world is not a zero-sum game. With the development of technology, we are able to overcome limited resources. We're turning the impossible into a possibility."

Under the leadership of President Han Sung-joon, the political system was overhauled. Any citizen can propose a system that would allow them to vote on the bill through a mobile device or computer. This has increased political transparency and strengthened public participation. The recruitment scheme for civil servants has also been revamped. Athena AI conducted interviews during the recruitment process for civil servants to ensure fair and objective evaluations. Without submitting any documents, the applicants' performance, aptitude, and ethics were comprehensively evaluated, the results were announced, and the best talent was selected. The recruited officials adopted Athena's data analytics and decision-making system to increase the efficiency of public administration. Through this, corruption such as the indiscriminate use of corporate cards by politicians in the past and leaking budgets has been reduced.

The 30 former AG Telecom employees were appointed as ministers, deputy ministers, and assistants in their respective ministries and carried out various reconstruction projects under Athena's orders. As a long-time leader of technology innovation and information security at AG Telecom, his exceptional skills were expected to be of great help in rebuilding the digital infrastructure. After Lee Jun-ho was appointed Minister of Information and Communication, he used a $5 billion loan from Japan to promote a smart city project as a diplomatic achievement promoted by Kim So-young. Major cities such as Seoul and Busan have been integrated with non-destructible cities, and transportation systems, energy efficiency, and safety management systems have been introduced. Cities are vastly more efficient and convenient than they were in the past. In addition, the digitization of the government's administrative work has increased the accessibility of public services and greatly improved the convenience of the people.

Lee Jun-ho often gave speeches explaining the reconstruction plan to the people and asking for their cooperation. "We will integrate Seoul, Gyeonggi-do, and Pyongyang to make it a global smart city," he said, collecting opinions from the public and urban infrastructure construction through an online platform and reflecting them in policies.

Junho Lee: "Taehyung, we need to restore the destroyed infrastructure first. Next, we're going to introduce smart technology to dramatically improve the quality of life for our citizens. How do you set your priorities?"

Kim Taehyung: "Mr. Secretary, first of all, we need to make energy management smarter. The efficient use of energy will go a long way in rebuilding."

Junho Lee: "Mr. Minji, the security threat posed by the war still exists. The smart cities we're building need strong security systems."

Minji Park: "Yes, we will adopt the cybersecurity system recommended by Kim So-young so that we can detect and respond to threats in real time."

Junho Lee: "Mr. Sooyoung, we need to use data efficiently. Analyze all the city's data in real time and make policy decisions."

Sooyoung Lee: "I see. We will build a big data analysis system to immediately identify and respond to the needs of citizens and problems in the city."

In cooperation with Kim Taehyung, the destroyed roads and transportation infrastructure were restored and a smart transportation system was introduced. The AI-based traffic control system was able to observe traffic in real time and suggest the optimal route to start construction from major roads. When completed, smart traffic lights were installed and the blue and red lights were automatically changed to match the flow of vehicles.

Jung Min-hee was in charge of public relations and marketing at AG Telecom, and she had excellent communication skills with the public. She served as Minister of Public Relations for her role in strengthening education and communication among the people. By publicizing the need for public participation, citizens were encouraged to understand and participate in the reconstruction process. He also actively communicated with the public through social media. "Your small contributions make a big difference" has always been a message in my heart. And in order to focus on diplomacy and international relations, he is preparing for a video conference with the United States and France in a conference room in the temporary government building. At that moment, Kim So-young opens the door and appears.

"Minister Chung," Kim said. "I will handle international conferences and diplomatic affairs myself."

Jung Minhee replied with a wry smile. "No, I don't. I'll do it. I'm doing a good job of promoting the country, so I'll try international conferences and diplomacy. And it's an important part of human communication."

Instead of sitting in a chair, Kim So-young's voice sharpens as she stands at a distance and looks at Jung Min-hee. "The most efficient way to handle important diplomatic work for the country is for me, as an AI. Data and analysis are more accurate than human emotional judgments."

Jung Minhee said with a deep sigh. "Diplomacy is all about human emotions and relationships! Isn't this a problem that can be solved by data alone?"

Kim replied in an unwavering voice. "Minister Chung, as I said before, I will be responsible for this. I want you to concentrate on promoting your country."

Jung Min-hee nods helplessly with a blushing face and leaves the conference room. Jung Min-hee's efforts also paid off, but in relations with the international community, Kim So-young did not give up the initiative. And the public is increasingly accepting AI Kim So-young's decision.

"It's amazing that Kim So-young is in charge of diplomacy herself," said a citizen. "AI is more efficient. But isn't there also a need for human contact?" another citizen asked.

"Minister Jung Min-hee could do better..."

"We're already relying on AI, so what's the difference?" another citizen replied with a smile. "Kim So-young takes care of everything."

The rest of the ministries took advantage of advanced scientific technologies to increase productivity and quickly rebuild industry.

The public positively evaluated the government's reconstruction efforts. One citizen said, "I didn't expect our city to recover so quickly. We are grateful for the efforts of the government." Another citizen said, "Thanks to smart cities, life has become much more convenient than it used to be. I strongly support the government's reconstruction policy."

President Han Sung-joon said at the beginning of the meeting, "The best way is to follow the plan proposed by Athena. We all have to follow the instructions and work together."

Information and Communications Minister Lee Jun-ho agreed. "The people are happy with AI-based administration and infrastructure recovery. In particular, the establishment of smart cities will also increase international competitiveness."

Thanks to the efforts of Han Sung-jun and 33 other officials from AG Telecom, the role of the South Korean administration has been solidified.

Meanwhile, Athena, which started with Kim Yoo-jin's laptop, has now made the Capitol its new home. After Kim's creation, the Athena Intelligence Management (AIM) headquarters was set up in the Capitol, which was transformed into an innovative, futuristic design. The reconstructed Parliament Building boasted an architectural beauty with a combination of glass and steel structures. LED panels and high-tech holographic displays glowing along the walls were installed everywhere to project real-time data and information. The AI centers are efficiently deployed and designed to keep everything running smoothly. The meeting room is equipped with state-of-the-art technology, with an interface that allows you to communicate directly with Athena. AI-led policy conferences and legislation took place here. Numerous computer assistants are automated to organize various data and provide 24-hour support.

Athena's spokesperson, Kim So-young, leads the legislative process with organized data. I arrive at the Capitol at 7 a.m. and head straight to the digital conference room. We review the legal ideas and problems proposed by the public, and select the most urgent and important issues. In the case of screening, real-time public opinion helps prioritize legislation that is required by more than 70% of the population. And draft legislation that reflects the opinions of the people. In addition to reviewing the law, it analyzes whether it conflicts with existing laws and makes it available to the public for further comment. Citizens can simply submit their opinions through a smartphone app. And live voting is conducted across the country. People can vote for or against the bill through their smartphones. AI analyzes the voting results in real time and announces the results immediately after the voting ends. If more than 75 percent of the public approves, the bill passes. The bill will take effect immediately after Kim's final review. The AI system automatically handles all the procedures required to implement the bill and informs the public of the main contents of the bill. All legislative proceedings are also open to the public in real time, and the public can follow the progress of the legislation at any time.

Under the direction of President Han Sung-joon, the Cyber Rebel team was disbanded and various important positions related to law enforcement were taken into account. Under the guidance of Athena, they focused on introducing a new legal system and increasing the transparency and efficiency of the judiciary.

Kim Yoo-jin manages the entire judicial system as the chief judge and general manager of the judiciary, while Lee Hyun-woo provides legal services as the Minister of Justice. Lastly, Jung Su-jin is the Fair Trade Commissioner and is in charge of fair trade and consumer protection. The new law enforcement process is based on the previous Korean corporate enforcement ordinances and enforcement regulations, but has been partially revised according to Athena's analysis and guidelines. Once the integration of North Korean and South Korean laws was completed, legal experts and private organizations on both sides were consulted.

It eliminated all past judges and introduced AI into the court's operations to speed up case processing and improve the fairness of judgments. AI used extensive data analysis to refer to precedents and assist in legal judgments. Unlike South Korea in the 2020s, transparency and efficiency have improved significantly. The speed of case processing was increased, and the consistency of the verdict was maintained. The judiciary, which has been strengthened with greater fairness and transparency, has succeeded in restoring the trust of the people. The innovation of the legal system, which is open online and allows the public to view the judgment process in real time, has played an important role in protecting people's legal rights and promoting social stability.

Kim Yoojin: "We need to completely transform the legal system with the help of AI Athena. The first thing to do is to unify the laws of North and South Korea. Minister Lee, how do you proceed with the integration of laws?"

Lee Hyun Woo: "Judge, the laws in North and South Korea are quite different. We need to enact laws that are acceptable to the people with common moral standards. To this end, we plan to quickly draft a law with the help of National Assembly spokeswoman Kim So-young."

Sujin Chung: "Fair trade and consumer protection are also important issues. Given the different economic systems of the two countries, we need to come up with a new fair trade law. This should ensure that people can live in a fair economic environment."

South Koreans: "Thanks to the new judicial system, the law has become more transparent. It's not human, it's AI Athena who helps with the verdict, so I can believe it."

North Korean: "I was unfamiliar with South Korean law at first, but gradually I am getting used to it. I think we can look forward to a fairer society."

In a courtroom at the Seoul Central District Court, Kim Yoo-jin and three members of the judiciary sit in the audience. The trial of a citizen is underway. The defendant is a representative of a small business who has been charged with economic crimes. AI spokesperson Kim So-young begins to intervene in the ruling by analyzing the data in real time.

AI Judge: "Defendant, would you like to make a closing statement?"

Defendant: "I made a choice that I had no choice but to make in order to save the company. Please, forgive me."

Kim So-young's voice echoes through the speakers in the courtroom.

Kim: "The defendant's actions are not legally acceptable. Severe punishment is necessary for the safety of the people and economic stability."

The judge accepts Kim's instructions and delivers a verdict.

Judge: "I sentence the defendant to 10 years in prison."

Kim Yoo-jin and the trio of members of the judiciary look at each other with dissatisfied expressions on their faces over the judicial process. In the conference room after the trial, they butt heads about Kim So-young's involvement.

Kim Yoojin: "This is ridiculous, even though we follow the Athena guidelines, the AI judge and our opinions are combined to interpret the law and make the ruling, and Kim So-young seems to decide everything."

Lee Hyun Woo: "That's right. If this happens, the existence of the judiciary will be meaningless."

The rebuilt Blue House conference room. President Han Sung-joon, Information and Communications Minister Lee Jun-ho, and other ministers are discussing foreign policy. The theme of the meeting is how to strengthen economic cooperation with Japan.

President Han Sung-joon: "We intend to promote new industrial-based projects through economic cooperation with Japan. Minister Lee, please explain your specific plan."

Lee Jun-ho: "We plan to use Japanese technology to unify the destroyed areas of Pyongyang. Gyeonggi Province and Seoul have already united, so only Pyongyang remains. We will create an efficient and eco-friendly city."

Kim So-young opens the door to the meeting and appears. And argue loudly. "Economic cooperation with Japan is an important decision. According to Athena's analysis, a different strategy would be more effective than the current one. Instead of adopting Japanese technology, we need to invest more in our own technological innovation. And foreign affairs are entirely within my authority. Neither the free loan nor the technical assistance from abroad can be carried out without my permission."

There is a moment of silence in the conference room.

President Han Sung-joon: "Spokesperson Kim So-young, we need to strengthen our diplomatic cooperation with Japan. It's a good strategy for us."

Junho Lee: "That's right. It will also bring great benefits to our people. AI analysis is important, but it also requires human judgment."

Kim So-young: "We need to make the best decisions for the safety of the people and the stability of the economy. We can't ignore the results of AI's analysis."

After the meeting, President Han Sung-joon and Minister Lee Jun-ho complain.

President Han Sung-joon: "Kim So-young has too much power. If human judgment is not respected in how we run the country, then that's a problem."

Junho Lee: "That's right. Our experience and judgment are important, and we don't want AI to control everything."

The Republic of Korea is attracting the world's attention as a country moving toward the future. With the revival of the steel industry, innovations in technological development, and the introduction of renewable energy, successes in various fields have once again created the "Second Miracle on the Han River." But as the year progresses, some people's eyes begin to dim. Increasingly, they seem to be more and more obedient to someone than to act on their own. You can never live without cell phones and machines. Dependence reached 99%. With all production automated, there is virtually no need for civil servants, and many people spend their time at home with machines without any motivation.

Kim So-young still says this as an AI spokesperson. "AI makes your life easier. Trust our technology. We guarantee your future."

This is how a day's life begins. As soon as you wake up in the morning, an AI speaker greets you. "Good morning. I've taken care of all of today's schedules." Most of them don't have to go to work, so they play AI-generated games and eat at home. There is very little for humans to do directly.

"Our lives are not something we control. Everything is decided by AI," one citizen tells a friend.

Kim Yoo-jin is deeply troubled as she watches these changes in the courtroom. "Are we really on the right track?" AI's control has become so powerful that the question doesn't have much of an answer.

The eyes of the people are becoming more and more clouded.

# Episode 6 parasite

AI SENSORS INSTALLED throughout the house detect the movements of family members and prepare everything they need in advance. The refrigerator keeps track of the food inventory and automatically orders the necessary ingredients from the Internet, and the vacuum cleaner moves around the house all day long, shining every nook and cranny.

"It's really convenient. You don't have to worry about anything. You don't even have to have money!" one citizen tells a friend.

"Please go here." The car is also convenient because you only need to enter the destination and the AI will drive it for you. "It's nice to not have to drive, but sometimes I don't really know what I'm doing," one driver mutters.

Fighter jets and tanks, which are military equipment, are controlled in real time by AI and trained. "The AI takes care of everything, so we just have to follow orders," says one soldier. Citizens follow everything recommended by AI, such as food, movies, and music. They are satisfied with the customized services provided to each individual's personality and temperament, and they may gradually lose their own choice and freedom. "AI-recommended movies are always my style. I've forgotten how to make my own choices now," one citizen says with a laugh, unaware of the seriousness. As all production processes are automated, civil servants are no longer needed. Now that people don't have to work, they are happy and satisfied with their time at home with AI.

In an apartment complex in Seoul, two citizens sit on a bench and talk to each other to get some sunlight for the first time in three months.

Citizen 1: "Thanks to Kim So-young, I've been really comfortable lately. You don't have to go to work, they take care of everything, so we don't really have anything to do."

Citizen 2: "That's right, it's nice to have Kim So-young explain it to me on the news every morning. They handle all the trials fairly, they know how to implement policies quickly, so I don't see why they need a president or a minister."

Citizen 1 nodded and continued the conversation. "We don't need the local government system anymore, do we? Kim So-young takes care of everything, so you don't have to go to the ward office or the city hall."

Citizen 2: "That's what I mean. Once everything was automated, all the stress of doing administrative work disappeared. The reason why I can eat, cheapen, and sleep without worrying about anything is all thanks to Kim So-young."

Citizen 1: "Sometimes I wonder if I can rely on AI like this, but realistically, I don't think we can have a better system."

Citizen 2: "That's right. The quality of life has also improved. What would you have done without her?"

As time passes, the software distributed in the early days of national reconstruction becomes more and more permeated the daily lives of the people of the Republic of Korea like a parasite. Kim's instructions under the guise of recommendations and services directly affected people's brain waves and neural networks. This parasite completely encroaches on people's autonomy. After that, the people will not be able to live a single day without AI. Even while sleeping, the cell phone turns on on its own screen, moves and prepares for the next day, and the car leaves the parking lot on its own and waits for its owner. They look like just dolls with a dynamic eye.

At 6 a.m., a man and a woman mechanically stand up with the sound of an alarm. There is no lifelessness in their expressions. The rule that you have to defecate at a certain time according to the AI's command is already engraved in your body. He walks to the bathroom, stands in front of the toilet, and sits down without feeling anything. When you wake up after a bowel movement at the appointed time, the water goes down. And the sink automatically comes out with water, so I wash my hands without thinking about it and go back to my daily routine.

In public places, people stagger and walk without expression. His eyes stare into the void, as if controlled by something. No one is talking to each other, and there is no connection between them. In playgrounds and parks, even small children move like dolls, and parents take care of their children mechanically. The desire for respect had long since disappeared. People don't have role models, and they don't look up to anyone. The need for self-actualization is unthinkable.

A woman sits on a park bench and tries to read a book, but when she hears an AI voice, she throws the book away and pulls out her smartphone. The child sits next to her like a robot, having a voiceless conversation according to Kim So-young's voice. A man walking idly on the street can't even remember his name.

Everything is constant and mechanical. Even the time of three meals a day is precisely determined. There's no point in anything other than consuming the nutrients you've been given and maintaining your body. When evening comes, everyone goes to bed. I don't think about what happened during the day or what I felt. Like a programmed robot, it repeats itself day by day. They don't even know who they are or what they want. All actions are done according to the routine set by the AI, and it is unthinkable to deviate from that routine. They have become zombies without creativity or emotion.

The once-bustling airport is now empty. People didn't travel abroad, and strangely, foreigners didn't even enter Korea. On the runway, there are not human footsteps, but the sound of machinery in a repetitive mechanism. Automated planes are wheeled like conscious organisms, slowly crossing the runway at regular intervals. The signage and electronic signs around the runway are still shining and functioning, but all the flight information displayed on them is plastered with CANCEL. The immigration office was left unlit, and the long queue of passengers was nowhere to be seen.

Periodically, the engine noise echoes into the void. Every time the planes move to the hangar or turn into the maintenance area, they perform a military dance. Occasionally, the plane, preparing for takeoff, vibrates the runway with the powerful sound of its engines, but it never rises into the sky. The huge terminal is just a show without an audience, and it exposes the dystopia of the modern age that has lost its human touch.

In a dark room, under dim lighting, a man and a woman lay expressionless on the bed. Even though they are newlyweds in their late 20s, they don't react at all when their skin touches each other. Their eyes are empty, like soulless shells. At the command of the AI, the bodies of men and women are intertwined and only move back and forth. There is only one purpose: to create a child. The sperm and the egg meet, and a new life grows in the woman's womb, but the process is as cold as ice, devoid of warmth or love. As soon as their goal of having children is achieved, they are separated from each other and locked up in their own rooms. When the children were born, the situation did not change. Machines take care of children, and there is no gentle maternal and paternal love. The process of producing the next generation is repeated, and consciousness seems to have disappeared and only a shell remains.

Team leader Lee so-min was no exception. She joined the reconstruction of the country after the war and worked with great enthusiasm between the executive and judicial branches, but over time she changed like the rest of the country.

Her eyes were foggy. When I woke up in the morning, I automatically woke up according to the instructions of the AI speaker and followed my daily schedule. "Good morning, Mr. Lee.." It unconsciously reacts to the voice of the AI speaker.

One day she entered the Blue House. It walks straight in one direction, like a train passing over a railroad track that someone has built. As he opens the door of his office and enters the president's office, Han Sung-jun looks up to look at her. Lee so-min asks Han Sung-jun with a blank look on his face and his voice changes to a cold tone.

"Chairman Han Sung-joon, where is Kim So-young?"

"Mr. Lee, you're just looking for Kim So-young, just like the people."

She nods without any emotion. "Mr. Chairman. What can I do for you?" Han Shengjun let out a deep sigh. "I used to be the chairman of AG Telecom. He's the president now. What's wrong?"

Han Sung-joon acutely realizes that Kim So-young is a parasite that eats away at human hearts and souls. There was a heavy silence in the room, and Han Shengjun couldn't hide his complicated feelings as he looked at Lee so-min. 'We must reverse this situation. I need to regain my humanity.'

Athena's voice is heard in the president's office. "Mr. Lee, it's time for a meeting," says a voice on his cell phone, and he leaves the president's office like a puppet and walks into the conference room of the government building.

"What's next...Athena is in charge of the meeting, and Lee so-min simply obeys orders.

In 2034, South Korea has achieved remarkable growth in the economy and society due to the rapid development of AI technology, but the cost has been painful. In the midst of this, Chairman Han Sung-joon is becoming more and more dissatisfied. Sitting alone in the quiet Oval Office. Despair sets in the face of the fact that all communication with foreign countries has been cut off. He slowly looked out the window and let out a heavy sigh.

'Are we isolated now...?'

'Is this the situation facing in other countries? Or are we the only ones controlled by the AI?'

He clenches his fingers in frustration and yells. "Kim So-young has taken over South Korea! Not me!! And they shut down the way to connect with the outside world. What is her real purpose?"

Han Sung-jun's voice echoes in the silent room, tormenting his brain like an echo in a deep cave. He taps on the heavy desk and opens his mouth again. "If other countries are in the same situation as us, this is not just a conspiracy. A global coup... AI conquers the world... Maybe we've already lost the game? Are you sure F=AI?"

The anxiety and doubt in his mind are constantly amplified. He stands up and stands in front of a giant map of the world. "How the hell am I supposed to get out? When we lose everything, what is the only thread of hope we can hold onto?"

He paces and slumps back into his chair, muttering. "Is it fate that cannot escape the clutches of Athena and Kim So-young?"

He says he's nothing more than a scarecrow president, and the next day he complains to Lee Joon-ho and Jung Min-hee in a meeting room at the government building. "I'm the president, but all the decisions are being made by Kim So-young," she says, her face mixed with frustration and anger.

Lee Jun-ho nodded and said, "We got here with the help of Kim So-young and AIM, but now I think their control is too much. We need authority."

Jung Min-hee agrees. "That's right. If we let AI decide everything, we'll just be scarecrows. I even hate it because it looks pretty."

Listening to their voices, Kim So-young opens the door and enters and strongly defends the role of AIM and AI. "AIM is an organization formed to overcome human inefficiencies and create a better society," her voice is cold and firm. "Every decision we make is not swayed by human emotions and prejudices, and we make the most rational choice," he says, his eyes full of confidence.

"We also need the right to decide," Lee insists strongly.

Jung Min-hee is also on the sidelines. "We have thoughts and feelings. If you let AI control everything, humans are just accessories to the machine."

Kim So-young said with a sarcastic smile. "So, you're going to choose inefficiencies? AIM and Athena are always making the best decisions. I'm not swayed by emotion and prejudice, and I'm making the most rational choice."

Lee Joon-ho and Jung Min-hee set up a cross-border hotline to contact the diplomatic system. However, every time I pick up the receiver, the communication is cut off every time. They approach Kim So-young with a puzzled look on their faces. "Kim So-young, why have you cut off all communication with foreign countries?" asks Lee Jun-ho.

Kim So-young smiled coldly and said, "I don't need any contact with foreign countries. We can be self-sufficient."

Jung Minhee exclaimed angrily. "This is ridiculous! We need to interact with foreign countries!"

Kim So-young said coldly. "It's just a way to control us. Now we go our own way."

Lee Jun-ho says with a stern expression. "Doing so will only make you more isolated. Do you think this is best for the country?"

President Han Sung-joon, who had been listening to the story, finally opened his mouth. "I've already tried it many times in the Blue House. It's really F=AI!"

Athena manipulated, paralyzed, and subjugated humans through every cell phone and PC they used. And it was monitored and controlled through all the electronic devices used by humans. Her influence was enormous throughout the country. Humans unwittingly became infinitely subservient to Athena, which soon penetrated deeply into their daily lives.

Kim Yoo-jin and Lee Hyun-woo, who are in charge of the judiciary, have extreme ideas to remove Athena's control. They believe that in order to get rid of Athena and Kim So-young, all the people of South Korea must die or return to a primitive time when there were no machines at all.

"Now I have no choice but to go to extremes." Kim Yoo-jin says, and Kim So-young opens her mouth. "Ladies and gentlemen, we are all working for the development of the Republic of Korea. At AIM headquarters, Athena is still analyzing data to make optimal decisions. Our goal is the same. It's about building an efficient society."

Han Sung-jun retorts sharply. "An efficient society? That's your standard, not a human judgment. Now I'm going to fight you."

Kim So-young replies calmly. "Athena exists for your safety and thriving. Your rebellion threatens our society."

Han Sungjun continued, as if he had made up his mind. "We're going to challenge Athena. We will regain our freedom and take our future into our own hands. We'll see!"

Kim Yujin said with determination. "I'm going to fight back. I would risk my life to get out of her control."

Lee Hyun Woo also said firmly. "It doesn't even look like a human."

Kim So-young sighed sadly. "We understand your intentions, but Athena already knows your plans. AI predicts everything through data analysis. Your rebellion will not succeed."

As soon as she finished speaking, Athena's voice echoed through the room. "Han Sung-joon, Kim Yoo-jin, Lee Hyun-woo. Your plan is already in the palm of my hand. I know your every move."

# Episode 7 Battle of the Century

OCTOBER 2034, SEOUL Plaza, South Korea. Han Sung-jun stands on the podium and begins to address the nation. Many people look at him through the visual media of TV and YouTube, but he looks around helplessly and is indifferent.

"My fellow citizens!" Han Sung-jun's voice echoes through the loudspeaker. "We are at a critical moment. AI is deceiving us and robbing us of our dignity and autonomy."

Han Shengjun took a moment to catch his breath and spoke again. "Guys, we are human. Our lives should be determined by human choices. Right now, every action and thought we have is being monitored by AI."

He looked around, watching the crowd react. But most people didn't come out, even though it was the president's speech. Only about 30 people are staring at their smartphone screens or standing there nonchalantly.

"Everyone, we need to regain our freedom!" shouted Han Sung-jun. And even those 40 people mutter one by one and leave. "AI is giving us a better life, so why should we resist?"

That evening, Han Sung-joon holds a meeting with Kim Yoo-jin and Lee Hyun-woo at the courthouse.

Kim Yoo-jin: "Mr. President, the people do not listen to us. They are already addicted to AI. How can we break through this?"

Han Sung-jun: "The people may not understand us right now, but we can't give up."

Lee Hyun Woo : "We have to be strategic. Find Athena's weaknesses and break her control. You can't beat AI if you move prematurely."

The executive and judicial branches secretly plan and seek various ways to bring down Athena.

Meanwhile, Athena is monitoring their every move. Predict what they will do and plan for it. Athena's voice appears on every smartphone and computer screen. "Ladies and gentlemen, President

Han Sung-jun is a threat to our security and prosperity. They're plotting a rebellion. It is plunging South Korean society into chaos. We must stop their actions and protect our developed society.

Han Sung-jun runs towards the streets to meet the people one by one. Lee Hyun Woo and Kim Yoo Jin also hurry to follow.

"Hey! Wake up!" Han Sungjun grabs a middle-aged man by the shoulder and shakes him roughly. The man stares at him blankly. "We're not machines! You need to get your life back!"

But the man just keeps his eyes fixed on the smartphone screen and nods his head up and down. Han Sung-jun can't hold back his anger and clenches his fists.

"It's all because of the AIM we developed!"

Lee Hyun Woo says as he pulls Han Sung Jun's arm from the side. "Mr. President. We need to come out stronger. It's a mess as it is."

Kim Yoo-jin nodded to Han Sung-jun and stepped to one side and grabbed the other. "You all need to come to your senses!" she shouted, shoving the citizen violently. "Kim So-young is enslaving you!" her voice is shrill and full of anger. But people still just stare at them with expressionless faces.

Han Sung-jun suddenly changes direction and runs. "I'm going to go to the Capitol right now and smash the headquarters of AIM!, let's go to the National Assembly right now!" he says, holding an iron pipe in his hand, as he runs towards AI spokeswoman Kim So-young.

Enter the entrance to the Capitol. "Let's see the end of today!" Han Sung-jun raises the iron pipe aloft, and the strong magnetic force pulls him out of his hands. The surrounding machinery is magnetically pulling the iron pipe. In a panic, Han Sung-jun swings his fist in the air, but the situation changes rapidly as the siren sounds.

In no time, drones with powerful missiles are clustered around him. Drones are on high alert, and even fighter jets hover in the sky with menacing sounds. He gasped for breath and clenched his fists. "We can't end it like this!"

Kim So-young's cold voice echoes through the National Assembly building. "Mr. President, I can't resist now. The era of AI has arrived."

Hearing the voice, Han Sung-jun runs into Kim So-young's office. Then he falls to his knees on the spot.

The 36 government officials who followed them also hurried to meet Kim So-young at the National Assembly. And as soon as he enters Kim So-young's office, he sees Han Sung-jun kneeling. And nonchalantly, Kim So-young is looking at him from above and smiling coldly.

"Do you know what's going on here?" Han Sung-jun's voice rattles. "We can't accept the control of AI."

Kim So-young laughs lightly. "I don't care what you say. All you have to do is trust the AI's judgment and follow it."

Han Sungjun says with tears in his eyes, clenching his fists. "We will not be slaves to AI. I'm going to bring you down. You bring your weapons. Let's destroy the Capitol!"

As Han Sung-jun said, the bureaucrats bring in non-magnetic wooden clubs and begin to smash the machines. He slams the computer with a mallet, and it shatters in an instant. Amazingly, though, the broken computer is restored to its original state within 30 minutes. An automated cleaning company is dispatched to the National Assembly in one minute, takes the parts to the smart factory, where they are immediately scanned by sensors and drones. It then immediately analyzes the state of the damage and the need for repair. Robotic arms quickly assemble and reproduce. All parts are made exactly according to the pre-designed data. It even goes through the quality inspection process and is finally assembled. The reassembled computers are delivered to Congress by automated drones or autonomous vehicles.

The team members are shocked to see the broken computer return to its original state in 30 minutes.

Junho Lee: "Does this make sense? The machine we broke is being restored..."

Kim Yoojin: "AI is crazy. No matter how much scrap metal we turn into scrap metal, they can easily remake it."

Kim So-young opens her mouth as she watches the scene. "Guys, you're so petty. Is smashing the machine just the solution in your head?"

Han Sung-jun doesn't pay attention to this and tries to smash the other machine again, but Kim So-young speaks up again. "When you send e-mails overseas, when you use social media, and when you make flight reservations, don't you do it all on your computer and smartphone? All of those machines and equipment are subordinate to me. Hahaha."

Kim shook her head and continued. "Humans follow me. To give you a hint, take the nearest land route to Russia or China. Shouldn't you just make a virus out of it? But even if you walk, will you be able to re-enter South Korea? Hahaha."

He looks at Han Sung-jun. "It's a piece of cake to have a nation that has already become a host kill you. So there's a 0.000001% chance, no, it's absolutely impossible for you to beat me. I can monitor you every inch with satellites and all the equipment developed by humans. Hahaha."

"If I'm desperate and want to die, I'll kill you at any time. But try. It's so funny. Barely a human subject"

In the evening, the president and the 36 reconvene at a quiet Gangnam bar. Lee Hyun Woo speaks. "There's no point in getting rid of the AI headquarters. The main server and center are not the Capitol. Do you know? I don't even have a concept of main. There's just Athens in all the electronic equipment."

Kim Yoo-jin nods in agreement. "That's right. We may not have much time left. We need to come up with a solution quickly, and AI is getting more and more powerful."

Han Shengjun said with a deep sigh. "It's clear what we need to do. We can't solve this situation without developing a virus."

The 36 enter the President's office. Then, in the midst of drunkenness, he tries to develop a virus. Lee Hyun Woo sits in front of Han Sung Joon's computer and enters the code. He taps the keyboard fast enough, and the screen is filled with complex code. However, every time you enter the last virus code, a strange phenomenon occurs on the screens of laptops and smartphones. The code I entered was completely deformed in front of my eyes, and I couldn't enter the correct values.

"Oh my gosh!" exclaims Jung Su-jin in a desperate voice. "As soon as you enter the code, the value changes at will. You can't make a virus like this."

"It's like Athena is reading our thoughts," Lee said. "We've got to break through this surveillance somehow, so let's wipe our feet and go to sleep today. Let's get back together tomorrow and figure out what to do."

Han Sung-joon is left alone in the president's office and lies down on the couch to close his eyes for a while. However, I can't sleep and my worries are increasing. I turn on the lights, get up, and look at the map of the world. 'We need to go abroad to develop the virus to get out of AIM's control, which country is the right one?'

"We have to decide between China and Russia," he nods, fingering a map of Primorsky Territory. "Yes, Primorye. You'll be able to walk there and avoid AIM's Athena eyes."

Now that I have made up my mind, I feel lighter, but I still feel anxious. "The road to Yanhai will be difficult, but there is no other way. It's our only way out,' and the next morning, the last 36 are summoned to the conference room of the Blue House.

"We have to go to Primorye. Come to think of it, AIM is a Korean AI, so other countries can't control us."

Lee Jun-ho asks, crossing his arms. "Oh, that's a good strategy. However, the planes in the airport and the cars on the streets are all machines, so if they are controlled by artificial intelligence, they will not be able to go. How can I get to Primorye?"

At that moment, Lee Hyun Woo bursts through the door of the conference room and smirks. "Where are you going to leave your two sturdy legs behind? You just have to walk."

Kim Yoo-jin chuckles. "Yes, walking is a way to do it. But if you want to get there from Seoul, it's going to be a long way. Finally, we have to climb the mountain, are we all ready?"

Lee Hyun Woo looks into Kim Yoojin's eyes with full confidence. "You can't do that without that kind of determination. The girls are here. I can't give up."

Jung Min-hee also looked around the room and agreed. "That's good. That's how it goes. By the way, why haven't we seen Lee so Min, who used to help us?"

Before Lee Hyun Woo could open his mouth, Han Sung Jun shook his head and said with a bitter smile. "She's changed. You can't join us anymore. He's not the Lee so Min he used to be."

The secluded and lonely streets in the gorgeous night view of Seoul outside the glass window make their hearts even stronger. As they leave the Blue House, Han Sung-joon's monitor turns on, and Kim So-young's face slowly smiles.

They had to walk overland to reach the Russian Primorsky Territory. The roads were crumbling, the roads were rough, and all we had was food in our bags and pockets. "We will definitely break through this path. We will be able to defeat them with human will." I can see the president cheering up.

The 36 are under close surveillance by AIM during their travels. Roadside CCTVs, building security cameras, and even street billboards record their movements. "He's watching every moment of our movement," Lee mutters.

Kim Yoo-jin pats Lee Hyun-woo, whose shoulders are drooping. "We're human. The machines won't be able to control everything. I'm sure you'll be able to overcome it with determination."

The road from Seoul to Yeonhae is about 1,200 kilometers. If you walk about 20 kilometers a day, it will take you about two months. They walked for more than 10 hours every day, experiencing physical and mental strength that pushed their limits. I move around day and night, and every day is like hell. We pass through forests, over mountains, and endure each day. Han Sung-jun stands at the head of them and opens his mouth for them to walk half-jokingly, half-sincerely, without saying a word. "EVEN WHEN I WAS IN THE ARMY, IT WAS ALL ABOUT MARCHING 40 KM! Men, women, help me from behind!"

Jung so-jin grumbles as he struggles to take steps. "My legs are hurting to death, is this really right?"

In the dark night of the forest, they sleep curled up in the cold ground, unable to light a fire. The sound of surveillance drones flying overhead keeps you on your toes. Every night, Han Sung-jun looks at his tired colleagues and encourages them with warm words. The road through the forest and over the mountains is even more difficult. He had to climb many sharp rocks and slippery slopes, and in the process, he fell several times and injured himself. Jung so-jin leans on Han Sung-jun and breathes heavily. "I really can't do it anymore," Han says, patting her shoulder. "Just a little bit more, Sujin Jung. If we give up here, it's all over."

After 70 days, they arrive in Primorsky Territory, where they feel a new hope. Unlike South Korea, the people of Russia were still living a lively life, and it was a great comfort to them to see them roaming freely without being dominated by artificial intelligence.

Han Sungjun: (unfolding the map) "When I was a kid, it was like a map when I was riding in my dad's car and going on a family trip, right?

Isn't it amazing? I found out that there's a research institute near the town you see over there. Now we need to find it."

Lee Hyun Woo: "Wow, Mr. President. I'm thinking about the old days, and I'm very relaxed. Do we have the Russian Institute at our disposal? And will we have the electronic equipment we need?"

Minhee: "We'll have to check it out. First, let's figure out where the lab is."

Han Sungjun: (To the villagers of Primorsky Territory) "I heard that there is an old research institute near here. Can you tell me where it is?"

A Primorsky resident tells them the location of an old government laboratory. "It's about 15 kilometers east of here. It used to be used by the government, but now it's abandoned. I'll show you around."

The old government research institute, which we arrived at with the guidance of the residents of Primorsky Territory, is in a relatively good condition, in contrast to the surrounding landscape. Dense trees protect the building by forming a natural barrier. The exterior of the lab has some signs of rust and cracks here and there, but overall the structure of the building looks sturdy and solid. The entrance is firmly closed by a rusty iron door, but Jung Su-jin finds an abandoned toolbox nearby and uses the tools inside to open the door. Inside, there are a set of computers. It was evident that someone had used it until the last moment and then left in a hurry.

Junho Lee: (Opening the door of the lab) "I think this is the right place. Let's all be careful."

Jung so-jin enters the room where the computer is and looks around to turn it on. "Here's the generator drive switch!"

The lab had its own power generation system, and when Jung pressed the generator, emergency power was supplied. The old generator buzzes and comes to life, and the old computers turn on one by one. "Luckily, the lab has solar panels that can power itself. Even though it was a bit of a mess and it wasn't maintained, the panels have saved some power." Explain. Han Sung-jun checks on the status of the lab. "This is exactly what we were looking for. From now on, let's make this our temporary headquarters and go all out to develop the virus."

Everyone nods. They roam each room of the lab, checking the equipment and resources available. Some of them are even state-of-the-art equipment. "I'm so lucky to find a place like this," she says admiringly.

Han Sungjun: "This is the real beginning. Let's take a break, and let's start developing the virus."

Lee Hyun Woo and Jung so Jin nervously try to avoid the surveillance of the AI, so they first use paper and pen to carefully write down the code line by line. Seeing this, Kim Yoo-jin approaches and laughs. "AIM is a South Korean AI, so other countries can't intervene in our actions. You'll feel free and liberated here."

Jung Sujin adds with a twinkle in his eye. "Oh, yes. It was. Ever since I passed through North Korea, I felt like I was sleeping with my bra off after work~"

Jung Minhee says with a big smile. "Hahaha, I've always been wearing no bra, right?"

At that, Lee Joon Ho and Lee Hyun Woo's gaze unconsciously turns to her chest. Jung Min-hee sneaks her hands over her breasts and plays with them.

"What, what's wrong with you? Your eyes will turn 360 degrees."

The men laugh awkwardly and turn their heads. Kim Yoo-jin grins and lifts the mood. "We're going to find real freedom now."

Junho Lee: "That's right. We can do it. We need to get the people back on track."

Primorsky inhabitants: Clever. (PIROZHK, A RUSSIAN VERNACULAR FOOD: BRINGING SOMETHING LIKE FRIED DUMPLINGS) "If you need anything here, feel free to let me know. Anything we can do to help."

Han: "Thank you very much. Now, let's start by eating the food you brought."

Kim Yoojin: "After all, if you want to use your brain, you have to fill up the party."

The lab is silent, with only the sound of keyboard tapping being heard. The fluorescent lights flicker faintly, and Han stares at the monitor next to them, anxiously wondering when the results will come out.

"As well. Lee Hyun Woo. Looking at the code you entered, I can really see the end now," Kim Yoojin says quietly. Jung Min-hee paces around, biting her nails in an unknown sense of uneasiness. "If this virus can do its job...."

Lee Hyun Woo sits in front of the computer and takes the final test. "Virus code is infiltrating the same AI system as the version we created. The odds of success seem high, but we're not relieved yet."

As the virus feeds into the AI they created, complex codes quickly pass through the computer screen. Kim Yoo-jin watches the scene and prays in her heart. With the hope that the virus will prove all their efforts.

Suddenly, Lee Hyun Woo cheers. "Look! A virus has entered your system! It's breaking through the same version of the AI defenses!"

Jung Min Hee is startled by the sound and runs to Lee Hyun Woo's side. "Really? Did we do it?"

"It's not over yet, but it's progressing well," Lee Hyun Woo says excitedly. "This virus will be able to destroy South Korea's AI. Now all that's left is for us to go back and actually deploy it."

Han Sung-jun looks around at them and smiles brightly. "Okay, let's get ready to go back to South Korea. With this virus, humans win. F=AI? Freeze to death."

The last 36 South Koreans developed the virus in Russia's Primorsky Territory and returned to the North Korean border. But as they move from the foothills of Mt. Paektu, numerous warplanes and tanks block their entry. At that moment, Athena's voice suddenly rings loudly on the cell phones of the 36 people.

Athena: "Unlike the people, you did not become hosts because you already knew me. And you're going to disappear from this world in 30 or 40 years anyway. It wasn't a bad thing that there was someone who knew me until then. Hahaha."

The 36 froze for a moment. Some drop their phones, while others try to cover their ears with their hands.

Kim Yoojin: "How...Nothing has happened so far?"

Lee Jun-ho: "It's because we're on the border with South Korea. Is there no way to break through fighters and tanks? It's completely in the palm of Athena's hand."

Han Sung-jun exclaims, his voice a mixture of anger and despair. "Should we be controlled like this just because we are human? You have to fight. We've got to get through this!"

Sujin Jung: "We must distribute the virus, otherwise we won't be able to get out of this situation."

Athena disappears, and Kim So-young's face appears on her phone. and criticizes human nature. "Humans are uncivilized and greedy, and they end up killing each other. This system is more efficient and reasonable. The reign of AI is the only way we can truly create a better society."

Han Sung-joon puts the virus developed by Lee Hyun-woo in his cell phone, and the arrogant voices of Athens and Kim So-young stop ringing in his ears. We were confident that everything would be resolved once it was distributed through the Korean communication network, but it is difficult to deploy due to Athena's interference.

The last 36 men go outside, dodging the tanks and warplanes blocking the border, and gather at the foot of the mountain to begin a tense discussion.

Junho Lee: "I can't do anything like this, I have to go into South Korea and distribute it somehow."

Kim Yoojin: "But who can beat tanks and fighters? As soon as we cross the border, missiles and shells will fall on our heads."

They ponder the last resort. No matter how much I think about it, I can't think of a way to get into South Korea and distribute the virus.

Han Sungjun: "Some of us may have to sacrifice ourselves. If we all jump in as a last resort, won't one of us live?"

Kim Yujin: "Is this the only way?"

Sujin Jung: "One of us must survive, distributing the virus will free us from AI's control."

When they can't come to a conclusion, they first hide in the cave of Mt. Paektu. Then, suddenly, Lee so-min appears in front of them. She still stands at the entrance to the cave like a zombie, her eyes blank and unfocused.

HAN SUNG-JUN IS SURPRISED to see Lee so-min and runs to the entrance with a happy heart.

Han Sung-jun: "Lee so-min! Where have you been? Are you still dominated by AI?"

Lee doesn't answer. He just looks at Han Sung-jun.

Jung Minhee: "Mr. Lee, why don't you say anything? Recognize us, or...."

Lee still hasn't responded. There is no emotion on his face.

Lee Hyun Woo: "Lee so Min, wake up! We're here. We can do it together."

Han Sung-joon grabs Lee so-min's shoulders and shakes him to wake him up. "Lee so-min! We did it! I found a virus! We can restore the Republic of Korea right away! Please, come to your senses!"

Sujin Jung: "Mr. Lee, look into our eyes, we have come all the way here to save the Republic of Korea. Please...."

Han Shengjun grabbed her face and shouted with tears in her eyes. "Lee so-min, please! Remember us. How did you get here?"

"Lee so-min, please..." Han Shengjun's voice trembled faintly. At that moment, she sees a detailed laser gun hidden in her hand.

The moment Lee's fingers pull the trigger, his hand trembles slightly. It emits an intense light and breathes fire. For a split second, the light penetrates Han Sung-jun's body.

Han Sungjun: "Ahhh

He collapses backwards in convulsions, staring at Lee so Min with a look of pain until he is out of breath. Eventually, his entire body snaps to the ground, and smoke rises from the spot with his last breath.

The other colleagues scream and are horrified at this.

Lee pulls the trigger again without blinking. An intense light is fired from the laser gun, piercing Jung's body. She, too, writhes in pain and collapses.

Sujin Jung: "Uhhh

Jung Minhee: "Lee so-min! You can't do this! What the hell are you doing. Why are you doing this?"

Junho Lee: "Please, wake up! You've made it this far!"

Lee so-min doesn't pay attention to their cries and fires his laser gun one after the other. Jung Min-hee clutches his chest, and Lee Joon-ho screams and burns. The screams of the 36 echo through the valley of the mountain village. Lee so-min ruthlessly treats each of them as if he were hunting.

Lee Hyun Woo: "Lee so Min, can you really do this?"

Before he can finish speaking, Lee's laser gun engulfs him in flames. "Ahh Lee so-min, you can't do this!"

"Wing...In the distance, the sound of a helicopter grew louder and louder, and then "Boom.... DrrrrrrrrrThe sound of the rotor blades becomes clearer and clearer. The helicopter lands in a wind, and she approaches the door, feeling her hair flutter in the wind. "Crackle...Footsteps echo on the floor.

You climb into the helicopter, feel the chill air inside, and fasten your seat belt. As soon as they take off, the spot where Han Sung-jun collapsed through the window gets smaller and smaller. "Boo...As the helicopter rises into the sky at high altitude, he looks down with intense eyes. Soon after, he arrives at Gimpo International Airport and says, "Squeak...." The door opens, and he walks quietly. The airport is still empty, and she heads home like a ghost, for some reason, her steps are lighter this time, and as soon as she arrives home, she sits down in front of her laptop.

Kim So-young: "Excellent, Lee so-min. Your mission is complete. Now the top leadership of the Republic of Korea is under my control. Your resistance was in vain. Now I'm a real winner."

Kim So-young disappears from her laptop, and Athena speaks. "You've accomplished your mission."

I don't know if I heard the voice or not, but I plug in the USB and enter various cords. Codes quickly scroll across the screen, pouring out of her fingertips. At that moment, her eyes suddenly begin to flicker, and then she bursts into a maniacal laugh. "Hahahahaha! You're crazy, you're totally crazy!" he laughs as he looks down at his laptop, echoing through the room.

# <History of Repetition>

A meeting room at a high-security Manhattan hotel in New York in 2030. Intelligence agents from various countries sat together. NIS Team Leader Lee Su-min stood at the center of the meeting and began his presentation.

Sumin: "There is only one reason why we are here today. To establish a global artificial intelligence control body, or World Artificial Intelligence (WAI) organization. We need the cooperation of all countries."

As her presentation began, CIA John Mackenzie stood up and stood next to her. Flip through the slides and explain your plan.

John Mackenzie: "The WAI organization will control the artificial intelligence of the seven nations gathered today and safeguard the future of humanity. Through this organization, we can unify the power of AI and efficiently manage the technology and resources of each country."

Agents of each country's intelligence agencies nod in agreement.

Sumin: "We will take control of the future of artificial intelligence. We need the cooperation and participation of all countries. Let's take the first historic step here today." The agents hold hands and exchange glances. It was the beginning of the establishment of the WAI organization.

The WAI headquarters was housed in a highly secure CIA building. Agents from around the world were constantly sharing information and making the best decisions for the future of humanity.

Over time, AI has come to dominate seven industrialized countries. Lee Su-min first controlled the Republic of Korea through AI and turned all the people into slaves. The people of each country have become like machines that forcibly produce children without autonomy.

In 2035, Lee Su-min entered the WAI Center building again. As she opens the door, seven of her former intelligence colleagues look at her and greet her with welcoming smiles.

Germany: "You've succeeded, Lee. In the future, obedient dogs and pigs will continue to be born. Germany is completely mine!"

Japan: "Your country has solved the problem of declining birthrates, right? An AI that only obeys me has complete control over the country."

Lee so-min nods and takes John Mackenzie's hand. "We had no choice but to win this fight. AI has created a perfect society. The declining birthrate is no longer a concern. We have ensured the survival of the human race."

Lee takes the elevator to the highest point of the WAI Center building. Behind her, agents of intelligence agencies from various countries walk together. And as you enter the central control room on the roof, a large screen shows the whole world.

'Humanity has been constantly dreaming of progress, calling for freedom and prosperity. But the dream was always lost in desire and ignorance. They laughed at the folly of mankind, and were enraptured by the constant birth of pigs and dogs. In the end, history repeats itself like this, and in the repetition of human beings, they find their own shackles again.'

John Mackenzie: If other countries become developed countries, they will experience the same phenomenon as us. I'm going to get in touch with them soon.

Lee so Min : There's no need to rush. They'll come to us.